FAIRY
CHIMNEY SODA

FAIRY CHIMNEY SODA

ERCAN KESAL

Translated from the Turkish
by Alexander Dawe

ANTHEM PRESS

Anthem Press
An imprint of Wimbledon Publishing Company
www.anthempress.com

This edition first published in UK and USA 2020
by ANTHEM PRESS
75–76 Blackfriars Road, London SE1 8HA, UK
or PO Box 9779, London SW19 7ZG, UK
and
244 Madison Ave #116, New York, NY 10016, USA

Original title: Peri Gazozu

Copyright © Ercan Kesal 2020

Originally published by Communication Publications
English translation copyright © Alex Dawe 2020

British Library Cataloguing-in-Publication Data
A catalogue record for this book is available from the British Library.

Library of Congress Cataloging-in-Publication Data
Library of Congress Control Number:2019949891

ISBN-13: 978-1-78527-149-6 (Pbk)
ISBN-10: 1-78527-149-0 (Pbk)

This title is also available as an e-book.

To the blessed memory of my father
Mevlüt the soda maker

CONTENTS

PREFACE

"All works of art rely on memory. Making memory crystal clear is how we make something tangible. Like an insect in a tree, an artist feeds like a parasite on his childhood. Then expending what he has gathered he becomes an adult, his maturity his final achievement," Tarkovsky said. I am of the same opinion.

I kept my glossy, yellow Avanos Public Library membership card cut from cardboard tucked away between my books until I started university. A genuine memento from childhood. With that card I could check out any book from that humble library and crawl into my hideout under my mother's loom where I would lose myself in the golden dreams of my youth, free of all the cares in the world. So I never actually chose one book or author over another. I couldn't tell the difference.

I dove into every book I randomly picked out with the same boundless curiosity and unquenchable desire ... Kerime Nadir, Jules Verne, Oğuz Özdes, Kemal Tahir, Abdullah Ziya Kozanoğlu, Nihal Atsız, Emile Zola, John Steinbeck, Victor Hugo, Reşat Nuri Güntekin, Ömer Seyfettin, Tolstoy ...

During my childhood and adolescence only two books were consciously (!) chosen for me and those were chosen by an elementary school graduate, a once farmer and then shop-keeper and soda maker, my dad Mevlüt. In fact the choices were made by an old book salesman in Kayseri:

The author of this one here won the Nobel prize this year. *Bridge on the Drina* by Ivo Andric; and this other one has sold a lot, the high school kids are always buying

it, *Red Cherry Tree Branches* by Reşat Nuri, take that one
too if you want .

Our lives are like balls of yarn we are forever winding, to
quote Henri Bergson. Our experiences trailing behind, we
are naturally gathering them up over time. For whatever we
experience along the way remains with us.

What we call "today" is but a collection of the past and
the future. In other words, the past isn't a period of time that
has slipped through our fingers or vanished into thin air. It
is something seated in the present, waiting. Every time I sat
down to write the stories in this book, I was startled to see this
sustained past as a "consciousness" that simultaneously encased
my "memories."

As if I had opened up a trunk in the attic and I was writing
down the memories each newfound object evoked. The more
I rummaged through the trunk the more I seemed to find.
And the truth is, the more I could remember of my past the
more I learned about myself. Every time I read my memories
of the past through the present, putting them down on the
page in the form of a story, I would surprise myself again and
again. My God, was I really the one who lived through all this?

It was as if I was making a video of the scenes as I wrote
them down. My goal was to write stories that would fully
expose the depth of my experience through powerful meta-
phor and objects that evoked universal themes of suffering;
stories that would provoke a personal reckoning.

So I struggled to capture an immediacy in my language.
I wanted the reader to "see" my stories, not just read them.
Something similar to a cinematic narrative technique. I have
always tried to show them the world and not simply tell them
about it.

Whenever I started a story I would imagine a fellow trav-
eler walking beside me on the journey as it unfolded. I would
try to "show" him or her whatever it was that I was seeing or
experiencing. And so my ideal reader is a friend who lends

an avid ear as he watches the plight of my protagonists, a true "companion" in feeling what I feel.

I don't know to what extent I have succeeded, but I have done what I know how to do, what is in my power. Sources of encouragement sometimes came in the form of a little note from a friend:

"My dear brother, today I could actually see what you wrote."

1
Kurban

... Ibrahim got up early that morning. He threw a saddle on the back of his donkey and with his son Ishak he set out for the spot that God had announced to him. At the end of the third day he saw it. He had made Ishak shoulder the wood for the sacrifice he was going to make. He bore a knife and the means to make a fire. They walked on a little. With the wood on his back, Ishak looked around and said:

"Father."

"Yes, son," Ibrahim answered.

"Here's the fire. The wood is on my back. But there is no sacrificial lamb. Where is the lamb we are to sacrifice, father?"

Ibrahim was silent ..."

★

Dad opened his first soda works beside the mid-neighborhood coffeehouse run by his friend Hafi. When Brother Hafi died of a heart attack in dad's arms, dad moved his shop to a place next to the fountain in the Lower Neighborhood. Later dad stopped making soda. After the death of his friend, he was haunted by fear and doubt for the rest of his life. Curled up under a blanket in the middle of the night with my eyes tightly shut, I would listen to his endless complaints, sometimes angry but mainly just helpless, as mom shuttled back and forth from the kitchen to their bedroom with a hot water bottle, trying to appease him:

"There's nothing wrong with you, Mevlüt ... You were like this the last time, and what came of it? Nothing ... It was just a cold ..."

Dad would keep on complaining for a while and then stop. For a few minutes mom would sit on the edge of the bed, unable to fall asleep, and then wrapping an old sweater around her shoulders she would sit down in front of her carpet loom.

The soda works shop was a cool, dark shop that smelled of essences. Just at the entrance was a little tub and there was a jug of syrup in a corner from which I secretly sipped and behind it was a globe-shaped copper cauldron. My older brother would turn me upside down and dip me into the waters. Thinking I might drown, I would struggle to get hold of his wrists.

Our hired hand Brother Dursun was always fighting with the women at the fountain. Once again they had unattached the hose that filled our storage tank at night.

"You're just giving us fountain water to drink and calling it soda," they say.

Now they weren't entirely wrong about that.

Hikmet's family lived in the boxy room above the soda factory and he was my best friend. His dad Şerafettin was a poor farmer who was lame in one foot. Hikmet was a quiet, dreamy boy. But he was great at math. He used to cut coupons out of newspapers and I was the one who most often completed the collection.

School is out for the holidays. It is a really hot day. Hikmet and a friend of ours are going swimming. But not in the usual spot: this time we are going to the Kızılöz shore.

On the bottom of the Kızılırmak there are deep depressions you would never think were there. People in Avanos call them *cumbak* and they are really dangerous. So after swimming for some time we were just getting ready to come out when Hikmet must have gotten snared by one of the *cumbaks* because he was sinking. Reaching out, he tried to grab hold of our wrists. We tried pulling him out but we couldn't. And before our eyes he disappeared.

I will never forget how his mother raced up and down the river with her hair all a mess, like she was out of her mind. It took them five days to find Hikmet. His mother spent those five days keening on the river shore.

3

It was on one of those days when I was going downtown with dad early in the morning when she saw us and came over. The grief had darkened her face.

"Mevlüt, Mevlüt ... The river won't give me back my child ... Look, your little lamb is here with you ... That's good but where's mine?"

I remember dad standing there, not saying a word.

★

On the Anatolian steppes spring is the brother of winter. On a Sunday morning I am getting the stove ready. This house is both home and a clinic. I rented the place last month. Finally I had got out of that hospital room I'd been staying in since I first came to town. I am really happy in my new home. The more I gaze at the sofa bed, fridge and bed I bought on installments from Kırıkkale, the happier I feel. The water heater is coming tomorrow. Brother Mevlüt sent over the stove from the clinic because they got central heating. The stove is practically new and it warms my place up real nice.

Below me is the meyhane where Hacı Taşan plays saz. Years later we went back to the place to shoot a film and the owner didn't recognize me at first. I showed him the picture on my driver's license without saying a word. And we embraced each other in tears.

After coming back late from the hospital and pottering about for a while, I finally drifted off in my armchair. When I got up I heard the village minibuses outside. It was already late in the morning. I went out onto the balcony. Turning back inside, I heard the prosecutor's driver call up to me:

"Doctor, we are off to do a *feth-i kabir*, the prosecutor says you need to come with us."

"*Feth-i kabir*?"

The prosecutor told me everything on the way there. There was a 21-year-old kid, the only kid in his family. Not more than a month ago he got caught up in a fight for no real reason and was stabbed in the stomach. Ok ... I remembered hearing about it. They had brought him over to the hospital in the middle of the night. There was nothing I could do for him so I sent him to Ankara. They operated on him in Numune. He was fine. But then he contracted an infection. And he died. They brought him back and buried him. But the matter wasn't closed. There was still the question of whether he had died from the stabbing or the infection. An opposing party claimed he died because of the operation. So the prosecutor requested a *feth-i kabir*. In other words, we had to open up his grave and do another autopsy.

We arrived at the cemetery. Everything was draped in the morning mist. In silence the villagers were planted all around us. Their hoca was waiting for us at the head of the grave. We would open the grave and when the autopsy was done we would cover him with talcum and bury him again. Five or six gendarmerie officers were lined up, waiting in front of the cemetery wall, just in case family members caused any problems. We pulled the body out of the earth and then the shroud. He was curled up like a fetus, resting there. On his stomach was the scar of a recent operation. Our job was done. With a prayer we buried him. The hoca, the technician, the official scribe and two gravediggers are present. In the distance the prosecutor is holding a handkerchief over his nose; for whatever reason he won't come over. I walk over to the car. Through the mist comes the low, sorrowful voice of a woman:

"Doctor, I am here . . . Prosecutor, I am here. But where is my lamb?"

Was this deeply heartfelt voice complaining or lamenting? Oh she sounded so much like Hikmet's mother.

★

On the morning of July 2, two sisters, Asuman and Yasemin, aged 16 and 19, were overjoyed: they were going to attend a festival in honor of Pir Sultan Abdal in Sivas. At the festival they were going to whirl. As if they were on their way to a wedding, they set off for Sivas. Just before events got underway Asuman called her mother.

"The whirling dervishes were wonderful, mom, all up above the ground like they were flying," she said. Concerned, Yeter Hanım said, "girl you must be drenched in sweat. If only you'd put a cloth on the back of your neck." Sometime ago her daughter had come down with pneumonia. Now how was her mother supposed to know that soon her daughter's lungs would be filled with smoke and the smell of burning flesh?

Soon after Asuman called her mother someone else from the group called her brother.

"They have stormed the hotel, don't tell mom, we're leaving the hotel and going to Ankara."

In any event it wasn't long before the mob outside had set fire to the hotel.

Their mother heard about it on TV.

"The names of the wounded and deceased ran along the bottom of the screen. I didn't know what to do. We went home. Everyone knew who'd died but they wouldn't tell me. I lost all hope. Somehow they'll find a way to call me I said to myself. But they didn't. For days I cried out for people to tell me where my Asuman and Yasemin were. But they didn't hear me . . ."

★

When the body of 15-year-old Hatice was found in Batman Creek last week, it was initially thought that she had drowned but it soon became evident that she had been raped and impregnated by two cousins and then killed by her two uncles with the encouragement of her grandfather. Hatice's body was in the State Hospital morgue till December 17. They simply left her there in a plastic bag, pushed into a cold drawer. No one came to claim the body.

The Batman Republic Prosecution Office announced that Hatice's body would be kept in the morgue for a few more days and in the event that no one came to claim the body she would be buried in the orphan cemetery.

Once upon a time there were tribes who lived in these lands that never buried their dead; instead they would leave the bodies on the top of a tower. The priests of the communities would hide somewhere nearby and watch to see which parts of the body the birds of prey would eat first.

This tower where vultures devoured the dead was called the Tower of Silence.

In Turkey we have ended up with a great tower of silence . . . We have turned our country into a tower where our tyrants can eat our dead.

Like mute priests lying low, we watch the fallen.

But I should finish my first story. After his son asked, 'where is the lamb?' Ibrahim the holy paused for a moment and then gave the following answer:

"God will give us the lamb."

I have an easier question:

"Who is going to put humanity back in our hearts?"

2

I Am an Orphan, Press Me to Your Chest

Faruk was the son of one of our staff members who kept working in our hospital even after he retired. He was a young lad in his thirties who was as thin as a branch. A quiet kid who kept to himself. His son was born in our hospital. That's how I knew him. Faruk then got cancer of the liver. They found it too late. It was already metastasized. The expert who administered the Doppler ultrasound was the one to break the bad news. Nonetheless they went ahead and operated on him, as the common phrase goes, "they opened him up."

Young Faruk worked for the municipality. He was married and they now had a son who was eight. A lovely boy with a blond head of hair. When his dad was in hospital I would often see him too. Whenever I went to check in on Faruk, I would find his little boy lying next to his dad, his head on his chest.

After the operation no one dared say anything about what had happened, no one dared tell him the truth. He was under the impression that the cancerous organ had been removed and that he was getting better. Meanwhile he kept asking his dad: "Now that you had the operation, show me malady. Bring me the malady so I can look at it."

His dad came over to me and awkwardly explained the situation. So we asked the operating ward and they sent over the piece of flesh wrapped in gauze—it was of no use to them anyway. His dad and I showed the boy the "malady." He looked at it for some time then leaned back comfortably in his bed.

But he looked a little perplexed: it turned out all that pain and suffering was caused by such a little thing.

Faruk died a month later. I went to his funeral. In a little mosque tucked away in the neighborhood. Only a few people attended. We stopped to pray together. Beside me were Faruk's dad and his little boy. He was praying too. He was just receiving his blessings and the prayers began again when the boy slowly went over to the body on the *musalla* stone. He approached his dad wrapped in his funeral shroud and placed his head on his chest. For a while the imam and the crowd looked dumbly at the child. It was as if his dad was still alive and in the most natural way he had placed his head on his chest. "He's an orphan now. What else is there for him to do," mumbled the neighborhood barber who was standing beside me.

★

Dad was also an orphan. Granddad died when he was five . . .

"Me and mother were in Kızılöz . . . It was July . . . Harvest time . . . The news came. Yusuf of the Cerit clan came with his horse and carriage to give the news, he told my maternal uncle Abdullah. 'Mustafa of Köse is sick . . . He's not well . . . They are taking him to Kayseri.' It was a summer day . . . Really hot . . . We set out along the path . . . Mother walked along through her tears . . . I struggled to keep up with her . . . Halfway there we ran into a horse and carriage and thankfully they took us the rest of the way . . . When we got there they had already buried dad. They said he started to smell, you see it was a summer day . . . Mother was in such despair as she cried because she wouldn't ever see his face again . . . . Water had gathered in the part of the courtyard where they had washed him . . . Water from the funeral cleansing . . . I was just a kid . . . With a stick I made channels so the water could run into a little puddle . . . I was playing on my own. Then my sister came over and hit me on the head . . . to say, 'look, your dad's dead and there you are making puddles'."

"What more can you remember about him, dad," I would insist.

"What kind of person was he? How did he treat you?" Toward the end, his mind was pretty confused and he would tell me fragments of memories:

"He was like this, dad had this broad, chubby face. And a beard. No doubt he got the nickname 'beardless' because we raised lambs and goats. In a cupboard in his room he kept sugar cubes. Sugar cubes. They were precious back then. I always had this really pale face. Everyone used to say, 'the kid's got worms, give him some gasoline to get rid of them.' So one day when I was playing on the doorstep, he said, 'Come inside and I'll give you some sugar. But first you have to drink this.' And he handed me half a glass of gasoline. 'Knock this back,' he said. And before I had the chance to spit the stuff out he stuffed a sugar cube in my mouth. I wept as I chomped on the cube. Then he pressed my head against his chest and we stayed like that . . . . I'll always miss him . . . not the gasoline or the sugar . . . but his chest . . . that's the only thing I remember . . ."

★

Dad was an interesting man. Although he was a farmer with nothing more than a primary school education, he had a unique relationship with knowledge and books. When I started middle school he was so happy when he could line up the books he'd brought in Kayseri on the simple bookshelf our uncle Huseyin the carpenter had made us. Ivo Andric's *The Bridge on the Drina*. My first book. The salesman recommended it, saying, "the author won the Nobel Prize this year." There was dad's crack at learning German from a couple that had settled in Avanos; the Olimpiya typewriter a friend had picked up for him on his travels abroad; and the adventure of opening his first soda works with his childhood friend Brother Yaşar.

★

Avanos. An evening in August. I am around eight or nine. The living room window over the garden is open. A warm breeze carries in scents from the garden. No one is home. I don't know why mom and my brother aren't there. I am lying on the *somya*, Turkish classical music is playing on our Philips radio. I am somewhere between sleep and consciousness. First the door opens like a shadow and then dad comes in. Leaning over me, he strokes my hair and then lies down beside me, puts his arms around me. I bury my head in his chest and fall asleep. In the most beautiful evening in the world, in the most beautiful house in the world, I drift into the most beautiful sleep in all the world. I never slept like that again.

★

The father of my childhood friend with whom I spent the whole summer fishing in the Kızılırmak and with whom I never hesitated to share my Tommix and Teksas comic books was an electrical technician who, when he was still a young man, fell off an electric pole and died. Both of us knew about it, but we both pretended like we didn't. There were times, especially when I was caught in the wrong while we were playing football, when I would break the pact with astounding cruelty: "You don't have a dad. You know that right? He's dead."

Speechless, my friend would pause for a moment then drop the ball and leave. Sometime later as I wandered around the garden with the ball in my arm and feeling as remorseful as a dog I would see my friend. He would be sleeping soundly on the divan in the entrance to their home, his head on his granddad's chest. Cocooned in such heartfelt silence. . . .

Neşet Ertaş tells the story of a "flat-chested" saz. Neşet asks his luthier, Hüseyin the Rabbit breeder, to make him a flat-chested saz. But Master Hüseyin won't do it. For whatever reason it just doesn't seem right to him. For the chest of a saz is always bulbous. So Neşet has his apprentice make him one. It's an incredible saz ... Later everyone else wants one just like it. Here is how Neşet Ertaş explains why he wanted a flat-chested saz:

"Over time the bust of a saz collapses ... When that happens the action on the fret board is too high. When the body is curved the lower half of the fret board is high, and the chest low.

When the chest falls there is a deeper, more heartfelt sound. With that in mind I asked for a flat-chested saz ..."

Our moral compasses have cracked. These orphans lost their fathers too soon, the chests upon which they once rested their untroubled heads have long since fallen. Have you noticed? When these chests fall the tyrants loom ever larger. And strings are stretched over our twisted and tangled pasts. Which is why the sounds we hear are so heartfelt and so deep.

Now let us remember the bequest of a Hittite king to his sons a thousand years ago in these ancient lands known as Anatolia where we now madly wage war and fail to make safe havens:

"When I die wash me gently, press me to your chest and leave me in the earth. That is all."

Well then how much longer will you sit and watch these sad orphans on your plasma TVs, longing for the chests of their fathers as they embrace coffins draped in flags? Or the anger of those abandoned, rebellious children whose relatives were not granted the right to be gently washed? Has it not been long enough?

3
What Has That Got to Do
with It, Dad!

In his usual calm and absentminded way dad walked up to the garden gate and stepped inside. Resting the tip of his foot on one of the jugs of water mom had lined up against the wall he washed his hands. Then drying them with the handkerchief he always kept in his back pocket, he went inside.

I'm reading on the *somya* in the corner of the room, leaning against the pillow mom knitted herself for her dowry. I can hear the sound of the centrifuge filling the garden pool with water. Mom is in the kitchen. In the air is the smell of something toasting.

My exam results have come back. I am going to study in the politics department. Ringing in my ear is that Cem Karaca song I listened to the day before in the Democratic Cultural Society:

This year the young brother is going to study politics/
But with no money for a coat he'll have to wear a parka, too.

As I mull over where I might find a nice parka, I have in my lap a book, *Deniz, Yusuf and Inan, Three buds in the Gallows,* which my uncle, an ardent supporter of Bülent Ecevit, had given me in the hope of, "raising my consciousness," to use his words. No matter where my uncle was posted due to his politics, he never tired of the food that was on offer in the far-flung corners of Anatolia.

Switching on our Philips radio, dad says with a dash of sarcasm in his voice: "Nothing will come of those people of yours."

I realize he is talking about the revolutionaries so I keep quiet.

"Last night when I was coming back from the club I came across your people writing slogans on the wall ... Two kids. I recognized one of them right away, Kadir, Ethem's son. There was a young kid with him. I didn't recognize him. He looked like Zelve, Faruk's kid. One was holding a bucket and the other one was writing. 'Down with Fascisim,' is what they wrote. I pointed out that they had made a mistake, put an extra 'i' between the 's' and the 'm.' Anyway, I told them and they fixed it. You don't put an 'i' there, I said. You still don't even know how to spell, son. How are you going to make a revolution?"

"What has that got to do with it, dad?"

★

I started life in Ankara like I was jumping into a color somewhere between black and grey. I was going to stay in the ground floor flat of a wretched, little apartment building on Süngü Bayırı in İç Cebeci. Two acquaintances from Avanos were living there. Both friends of my brother. One of them was a soldier in Mamak, a reserve office, who only stayed there over the weekend, and the other was a Railway engineer. Although the door only opened halfway, we managed to squeeze three mattresses into the front hall. Near the apartment was the Kütahya Dormitory. Supposedly the Nationalists stayed there.

Across from the dorm the man at the corner shop raises his chin at an overly made up middle-aged woman buying cigarettes and says to my brother, who is helping me move a few pieces of furniture brought from Avanos in an Anadol truck:

"If only it was night and we could hop in bed." My brother laughs. The shopkeeper is from Tokatlı and my brother assumes he's a leftist.

"Those ones over there are Kurds," says the shopkeeper, referring to the students in the dorm. He looks me in the eye as if he's trying to figure out where my brother stands on all this and then waves his hand to say "forget about it" and he goes over to the pastas. But we can still hear him:

"You might be a Kurd or you might be for Ecevit, doesn't matter to me. We only care about our putting food on the table."

Dad and I are climbing the stairs to the Politics Department. They searched us seven times before we actually got through the door. I had this sinking feeling in my heart. Dad is looking suspiciously around the room. The walls are covered from top to bottom with slogans and placards. Someone who says he is a representative of the association comes over to us:

"Welcome, friend."

Together we walk over to the registration desk. Dad is startled, unsure if he should follow us. The representative is just a kid who's acting like dad isn't even there. At one point dad leans over, giving me the impression he might say something to the kid.

"Uncle, you can get going if you like. There's no need for you to wait ... Your son is in safe hands here. Don't worry. Alright?" he says before dad can get a word in.

Dad waits in a corner until we finish with the registration. Then I go over to him. He takes some money out of his pocket and hands it to me. He pauses and says almost in a murmur:

"Son, look after yourself. Don't get tangled up in everything ... I just don't understand this behavior. These kids have no respect for their elders. It's their way or the high way. What kind of revolution is that I have no idea?"

"Dad, what has that got do with it, for the love of God?"

And then there's Izmir ... I am studying medicine. Dad gets off the bus in Bornova. He's coming to see me with *pekmez* mom asked him to give me ... The dormitories are now in the hands of revolutionaries.

"We are providing our own security!"

Those on guard have given dad a hard time before letting him through. He looks at me in surprise. The dorm is now under our control and that night he is staying over as a guest. After he's taken a shower and changed, we go down to eat in the cafeteria. He keeps glancing left and right. In the morning he'll take the bus back to Avanos. Leaving the dorm, we walk side by side down the long road lined with olive trees that leads to the gate. I know what's running through his mind: "Is my son really going to be a proper doctor?" He is troubled. I kiss his hand. He hugs me. Unable to hold back the words, he says:

"Son, what's going on here? I can't tell if these kids are students or soldiers. They all have ashen faces. And they are all dressed in rags. They don't look after themselves. Always smoking cigarettes, drinking tea. How are these kids going to change the country, how are they going to make a revolution?"

"Dad, what has that got to do with it?"

Then there was the coup. We didn't know what hit us. They threw us all out of the dorm. Now there's no place for us to stay. I can't stay with my friends. For two or three months I sleep in the bus terminal. Some time after that I go home. Dad has moved my bed away from the window in our house in Avanos. He thinks that someone passing by on the street could easily shoot me to death. Now there is no turning back on our chosen paths. When we see our enemies we charge like bulls chasing the color red. No one guns me down on the street but someone provoked by a local machine guns the coffeehouse where a friend of mine always hangs out. Projectionist Orhan, who rolls all the best films, is killed. Most of my friends are on the run. We have become birds without a nest.

It's like that line from a poem by the Iranian poet Forough Farrokhzad, "someone wrote the word stone on a wooden board and all the birds in the courtyard took flight."

In those chaotic years I graduate and then sign up to do my mandatory civil service. Dad is happy but now I really am a doctor. It is my seventh year in Anatolia. I need to be in Istanbul. I want to be posted there but they won't make it happen. It is clear what dad is thinking: "Son, you have a thick file. Don't you think the ministry knows what you have been up to? You should have left all that behind, son."

I resign and leave my work. Now I am in Piyalepaşa in Istanbul. I have turned a repair shop into a hospital. Dad is much older and he has Parkinson's disease. He and mom are both living with me. He loves sitting with me in my office in the hospital and chatting over coffee. In those days I get caught up in politics. In theory this is now "realpolitik." I am racing about day and night. There are dinners, ceremonies and parties. My room is always overflowing with people. I am going to be a Reis Bey, a distinguished chairman!

One day party delegates come to see me and only dad is in my office. Of course they don't know who he is. I am speaking with someone in the room next door. Some time later I come back. The delegates have left and dad is disgruntled. He says, "Son, when you were in the other room those people wolfed down all the biscuits on the coffee table. Meanwhile they were saying things like, 'eat 'em up, buddy, let's eat all the doctor's biscuits. Does the doc think it's all that easy being a municipality mayor? He's got to cover the costs.' Son, no good will come of those people. They are just out to fill their own bellies. How are they going to feed the nation?"

This time I didn't say it: "Dad, what has that got to do with it?"

Dad went through some trying months before he died. I always did my best to be with him. I knew I was going to lose him soon. He would ask me all sorts of questions and I would try to bring up subjects he liked.

"What do you think about this? What's your take on that?"

"How should I know, son? I have all these memory slips, son ... But I trust you ... You have never done wrong ... you know what's best."

Not much later I lost him ... My heart ached ... Indeed now I really needed to say those words that for so many years were a call of protest.

"Oh dad! What has that got to do with it, for the love of God? How should I know? Now more than ever I need to hear what you have to say ..."

4
I Am Grown Up, Dad

I am going to middle school. So I must be around 11 or 12. It's a strange time. Dressed in caps that make us look like soldiers we salute the *kaymakam*, the garrison commander and our teachers when we pass them on the street. Going downtown at night or to the cinema, such places are forbidden. Selected upper-class kids with armbands are always patrolling the streets and we were busted the moment one of them spotted us. The following morning after the flag ceremony and before the first class we have to brace ourselves in Riza Bey's office. That morning's victim is waiting for the teacher and the entire class and the staff from the headmaster's office, his cheeks flushed bright red, his young body squirming from shame. Among the memories of village schools is always the teacher who beat you the most and how often and with what. The happy memories are so few they are hardly even remembered.

It is Sunday and there is bathroom panic at home. Anyone who goes in accuses the person coming out of finishing all the hot water. Dad is stretched out and asleep on the mattress beside the window overlooking the garden. On the divan in a corner of the living room I am reading but also keeping a close eye on what is going on around me. I am in a good spot. In my lap is a book I got from historian Ibrahim: *The Death of the Bozkurts.* I'll finish it tomorrow. I have noticed that my brother has *I loved a Girl in High School* but he won't give it to me so I need to find some time when he isn't home.

As my ebe lays a blanket over dad, she wakes him up and he angrily tosses the blanket to the floor. In a huff she complains to mom who is passing by with an armful of wood:

"Snow falls over those who fall asleep, my lamb. I was just covering up the boy so that he wouldn't be cold."

"Come on, your turn for the bathroom. Everyone needs to wash, and I still have so many other things to do," said mom when she saw me. Helpless, I put my book down and went to the bathroom. Locked the door behind me right away. I got the water warm as I kept my ear tuned to the door. Now mom would come to wash my head with soap. Mumbling something to my ebe she came to the door. Not thinking that I might have locked the door, she tugged on the handle a couple of times. Silently I am waiting.

"Open the door, my lamb."

Waiting a little more and gathering up my courage:

"I can do it myself, mom."

I feel her pause for a moment.

"I'll just soap your head, then you can do the rest."

"I'll soap it myself, mom. I can wash myself now, you go."

It feels like I can see her look of surprise on the other side of the door. Then she puts something down by the door and leaves. I hear the glass door that opens onto the living room close. Yes, now I am alone and I can wash myself on my own. I am grown up!

★

August. I have passed the exams that will grant me free board. I am going to the High School in Niğde. Now I feel like a guest at home. Sitting on the edge of the pool, I am eating a tomato I have plucked right off the vine. In the air there is the scent of evening primrose flowers. I am wearing a light blue shirt with short sleeves. I bought my jeans last year: real Wranglers! I am all crisp and clean. The wind off the steppes starts at my feet and then makes its way up the rest of my body—this wind can make a man shiver—and I feel washed one more time by the wind as it rises off the top of my head and reunites with the air. Savoring the sharp tang of the tomato in my mouth and thinking that I might go back into the garden and grab another, I hear a song wafting out from the open-air cinema. They are playing Şükran Ay's, "I couldn't love my dark-eyed one." This is the last song before the film starts. Hurrying out onto the street, I start to run. Truth is there are still the teasers before the film starts but I need to get there on time.

Holding a Tekel beer, the film machinist Brother Yavuz is explaining something to someone at the door. Good, so the film hasn't started yet.

Not many people are here today. Soon a black and white film hits the screen. It is a strange one. There's a man, a painter, who is in love with a woman's portrait. The woman says, "What are you going to do with my portrait. Here I am standing right in front of you, love me." The man says something like, "Don't get between me and my portrait." Later they both die. Wide-eyed, I watch the film. Leaving the cinema and heading home, I walk along the dark roads and there is a strange flutter in my heart. I think of the girl I'm in love with. Then I think of mom, dad and my brothers . . . Then how my face looks in the mirror and my body that is always changing. It feels like there are things in this world I know nothing about and it occurs to me that life isn't something so easily understood. What's happening to me now? Growing up isn't easy . . .

★

We are going to a village quite a way out of town. It's winter. It takes us some time to get to the house where the funeral is being held. The villagers have gathered in the courtyard, waiting for us. A young woman has shot herself. I am about to perform my first autopsy during my civil service as a doctor. Leaning over the woman's body laid out on a wooden plank in the middle of a mud brick storehouse, I am trying to remember my notes from med school. First the cranium. No, first I have to write down what she's wearing, her height, approximate weight and appearance. Then I should take off her clothes and move on to the standard autopsy. When the prosecutor leaned over to offer me a cigarette, I was caught repeating the sentence, "three sections have to be opened." Oh my God, I hope everything goes all right. I'm aware that the autopsy technician is keeping a close eye on me. Anyway soon enough we were half way through. But there's still no bullet: we can't find it. There's an entrance point but no exit. Which means it has to be in there. The short, stout prosecutor keeps coming over to me and asking. Clearly this is going to take a lot longer if we can't find it. The technician pauses for a moment and then makes a philosophical statement about the missing bullet:

"It can see us, hocam, but we can't see it, you know that right?"

In the end we have our eyes on the bullet, too, and pulling it out we finish the autopsy. The prosecutor is really cold now and keeps hopping up and down. But he is delighted when we find the bullet. Yes, now we can move on to his part of the job: typing up the report. Spitting on his fingers, he rolls a piece of carbon paper into his Olimpiyat typewriter and starts tapping out the official report:

"Ercan Kesal, born in 1959, son of Mevlüt, was taken into our custody and duly swore to determine the cause of the death ..." Cause of death? Was I supposed to tell him? How in God's name was I supposed to know why this dark, thin-faced girl in a faded dress and ripped sandals killed herself in the middle of this strange land that was not unlike some dim planet, the source of such heartache? But you see I had to give an answer. Because I had grown up, I was a doctor.

★

The nurses who see me pacing outside the door to the maternity ward say, "You can go in, too, if you want Doctor." I drive away the offer with a shake of the head as if I am used to such a situation. But inside I am a tangle of nerves. I have to keep up appearances. Meanwhile I study the faces that come out of the operating room. Has something happened and they aren't telling me? It feels like a thousand years have passed when they bring him over to me in an incubator. Thank God everything is all right. I look at his long hands and feet. He looks like me. His mother has woken up from the anesthesia and she wants to hold her baby. They place the little boy who isn't much larger than a hand on her chest and when she lifts up his head and looks at his face she says: "Is this mine? Is this my baby?" Then with tears in her eyes she gives Poyraz to her mother who is looking down on them. "Look, mom this is my baby." The joyous tumult in the room sucks up what her mother says like a vacuum and then the full weight of her words falls on my heart:

"Ah! My baby girl. My baby girl is now a mother. She's grown up to be a mother . . ." And so my wife is a mother, too, she is all grown up.

Now we are in Istanbul. My son is seven years old and he's a real live wire. When we are alone together, I always keep an eye on him, if only out of the corner of an eye. Sometimes he gets into some dangerous situations and this worries me. The other day I notice him going into the bathroom while I am working. There is something in his hand. Getting up I silently go after him. The bathroom door is ajar. Through the crack I can see what he is doing. For a short while I watch him. He is filling a bag with something and taking something out. Suddenly his head turns and he sees me. I am caught. Opening the door all the way he says with resentment in his voice:

"Dad, you need to stop being like this, I'm grown up now."

Silently I go back to my room. My son has told me 'I have grown up.' Which means I can die . . .

5
The Weight of Your Coat

The 1970s and I'm in middle school. Probably a Saturday. All day a little truck drives through town playing an announcement from a loudspeaker that echoes over the steppes: "Come one, come all. Neşet Ertaş and surprise musical guests performing tonight in the Avanos Yeni Cinema. Tonight in our cinema, Neşet Ertaş!" Though students were forbidden to go there at night, I always found a way to get in. And I just have to see Neşet Ertaş. My usual ploy does the trick: I go into the cinema with a case of soda and I stay put. The place is packed to the gills. My uncle and his friends are sitting up front so I have to keep out of sight. I plant myself somewhere in the back and eagerly wait for Neşet. First come the musical guests, a woman and a middle-aged man sing musical arrangements. Not many people seem all that interested. The musicians are quick to finish. My eyes are glued to the wings. Someone comes out and places a wooden chair in the middle of the stage. A little later Neşet walks over to the chair with his saz pressed to his chest and his shoulders hunched. In his suit and his bright pointy shoes and his Ayhan Işık mustache, he is still a young man. Taking a bow, he sits down. He sings two or three folk songs. The crowd is up on its feet. But Neşet looks a little uncomfortable. He stops and says those words I would hear 40 years later in a open air theater in Istanbul:

"I am the ground beneath your feet, a slave to your hearts. So allow me to take off this jacket."

Taking off his jacket, he drapes it over the back of the chair. Now he's free.

His voice becomes one of the most beautiful the audience will ever hear.

★

Days just before the 1980 coup. Winter. A foul wind is blowing and everyone is at home or huddled in the coffeehouses. The 19th of February. It is the anniversary of the murder of Ulaş. We're preparing for an illegal political rally in town. In the evening we'll light tires and give speeches. We're going over the plan. The kids have found several truck tires and they are wheeling them over now. Everything is ready. I'll start chanting the first slogan:

"Brother, Ulaş! Your blood was not spilt in vain!"

Then we'll roll the tires over to the statue in the square and set them on fire. And then, and then it's up to God. We haven't been all that discreet because the police have already picked up on us: they are "standing by." After the evening call to prayer, we leave our meeting point and start racing toward the only public square in town. The police chase us before we even get to the chanting and the burning of the tires. Like baby partridges, we scatter in all directions. I sharply turn into a narrow road leading up a hill. Someone is right on my heels; if he reaches out, he'll have me. He's shouting:

"Stop running."

The street gets steeper and though he is overweight he has no intention of letting me get away. Suddenly he has the back of my jacket. We both keep running. And I slip out of the jacket, leaving it dangling in his hand. I feel lighter as I fly up over the hill. Out of breath, he watches me go, holding onto my jacket. Speeding around the corner, I am gone. Now I am free.

★

It makes me angry to look at that old hospital jeep. It's out of gas and we can't get out to the villages to administer vaccinations. All our requests for gas are rejected. Dressed in a turtleneck, the local mayor comes to the ceremony for the April 23rd

Children's Holiday and he is defensive with me—indeed we were never on good terms. But why? The accountant tells me: "That's not it, doctor, no other civil branch gets gas. It seems to be a matter of security, at least that's what the commissioner kept telling me the other day."

Chatting in the local club one evening, the agricultural minister tells me that their veterinarian is going off in the same direction to inoculate the dogs the next day. "Why don't you hitch a ride with them?" he says and I jump at the offer.

In the morning I am standing next to health officer Erdinç, who is holding bags full of vaccinations, waiting for the agriculture minister's Renault to arrive. Soon the car pulls up and I squeeze in beside an assistant in the front and the health minister makes it four in the back. During the journey, I keep shifting in my seat, always addressing the veterinarian as "doctor."

When we arrive in the village, the vet and his team are welcomed in a big courtyard at the village chief's home and we are taken to a classroom at the elementary school. There we begin waiting for the children. In the first hour we only manage to administer shots to the teachers' children. No one else. I step outside and look around. There's a long line outside the village chief's home. All those village dogs. The vet has a lot on his hands. I send the health officer to the local mosque to ask the imam to make an announcement over the loud speaker. One of the village chief's daughters comes over with a young boy, who is a village guard, but no one else.

Toward noon I start wandering through the village. It is harvest time and almost everyone is out in the fields. Everyone is working, save those tending to the dogs. I set my sights on a field full of children and launch my attack. A dark-haired boy, about six or seven, has no idea what's going on. Sweeping him up into my arms, I head back to the school. The technique works. I take Erdinç with me on the next trip out. By then the other kids have heard about us and they scramble the moment they see us. We deploy hunting tactics: Erdinç rounds up the prey and I bag them. As we tackle them to the ground, mothers and fathers silently watch us from a distance. Clearly they have decided to stay out of it. Within an hour we have captured and immunized nine or ten kids. But the remaining few will be the hardest. They are a little older and wiser to our game. I can't remember how many trips I have made when I step into a large field, a little stream running beside it. I spot three of them. If I chase them toward the stream, I can corner them there. Erdinç gets a grip on two and leads them away. But the last one has some wheels on him and he bolts. At one point I get close enough to catch a piece of his old jacket. I feel a rush of joy as he squirms out and then he is gone. I'm left there holding nothing but his jacket. Scrambling up a hill without breaking his stride, he is the image of a lizard that has just lost its tail.

★

I always remember the way dad used to straighten his jacket collar in the mirror. He loved suits. Whenever his tailor Celal got some good fabric, dad would ask him to make him a new suit, or at least a new jacket. In his suit and his white hat and his shiny shoes, he was the perfect town soda salesman. He had only finished elementary school but his nickname in the city club was College Man, and, although he always kept it a secret, I think he really liked it.

"Your father was just the same when he was a farmer, sweetie," explained mom, equally proud and disapproving. "He'd go to the club and sit down with the teachers and the local prosecutor. It made your uncle furious. He'd say, 'Sit with the other flat soles! What business do you have with those shiny shoes?' But your dad never said a word, just did what he thought was right."

By then I was in Istanbul and only made it out to Avanos for the holidays. Each time I noticed how dad was slowing down, and spending more and more time in bed. On my last visit, I brought him a fancy jacket, something I knew he would really appreciate. He put it on early in the morning and, trembling, he stood for some time in front of the mirror. Parkinson's Disease had taken its toll; he was practically swimming in the jacket. Unembarrassed, I said, "Look at that, I got the measurements just right. A perfect fit." In that jacket draped over his little body, he greeted all his guests and sat down to chat with them, and he kept it on until I left for Istanbul. When I went to say goodbye on that last day, he said:

"Son, this really is a beautiful jacket but it's a little heavy. I can't wear it anymore. Could you help me take it off?"

My dad could no longer carry 90 years of the world on his shoulders.

I helped him out of that jacket. And he never wore it again.

6

"We'll Ask Someone for Our Name, and She'll Tell Us"[1]

S ummer. We are in our two-story stone house in the lower neighborhood. The ground floor is a stable. But this is a big house where we live with our aunt and uncle and our cousins. You go inside through a heavy old wooden door. Three steps later you are standing in a broad courtyard. At the far end of the courtyard is a cool dark cave called a *tafana* that I always imagine is much deeper than it really is. In the middle of the *tafana* is a pole. There is always something hanging from it that looks like a leather pouch. The plump, pink body of a lamb. Stuffed to the brim with fresh white cheese. Anyone passing by can casually plunge a hand into that miraculous pouch bursting with an endless supply to get some filling for a sandwich. In one of the dark corners of the *tafana* there is a little grotto with baby lambs. Hopelessly bleating they are always trying to get out. But that day the place is steeped in silence. Nobody is home. Dad and my brothers are at Kızılöz. It is harvest time and all our animals are on the high meadow.

Mom is sweeping the front of the house with a twig broom. The only sign of life on the steppes seems to be the dust swirling up in the air. I am reading a book in the hollow right behind the loom that is in the hall all year round. This is my secret hideout. The mesh of the carpet on the loom makes the perfect shield for my little hideout. Everyone at home knows where I am hiding throughout the day but they keep quiet

---

1. A line from a poem by Turkish poet Edip Cansever.

about it. I drift off and then wake up and pop my head out when I'm hungry. At one point I slip into a dream, my book in my lap. I come to when I hear the rhythmic tapping of a walking stick on the little floor stones. The sound comes closer and then stops outside. Someone is talking to mom. She comes inside and when she comes out of the kitchen with a jug of water I slip out from under the loom. Now I am on the door-step. Before someone I have never seen before: an old woman who can hardly see straight. She sits down on the stoop, leaning on her stick for support. Slowly she drinks all the water mom brings her. I watch water run out of the corners of the jug and look at the tiny patterns it makes on her tattered, dusty, brightly colored cotton veil.

"Let there be many like you who give out water, my lamb. Let them be spoken of on the lips of the past," she said joy-fully. As mom leaned over to take back the jug the old woman slowly took her by the wrist:

"What was your name, my lamb? Who do you belong to? Whose family are you from?"

"I am from the Köse family," said mom calmly. "The bride to Mother Cemelli."

The old woman paused for a moment and then spoke as if her mood had brightened:

"Is that so my lamb? So then you are the daughter of our butcher Haci Mehmet. Good job, my lamb! You have earned your keep! Good on you! So that's how it is. When someone asks your name don't give your real name. Give them the name of your mother-in-law. That way you won't have any problems."

Truth is I had no idea why it was a good thing for mom not to have her own name. Bewildered, I went back to my hideout and my books.

★

On Thursdays there is a street market in town. Right outside our front door is Armageddon all over again. As usual Kasım is screaming and shouting at the patients. But no one is paying him any attention. The patients he is trying to coerce with some authority are all his neighbors. Later that evening they will drink tea on his doorstep and shoot the breeze. But now all this looks more like a makeshift play, people screaming and shouting then suddenly bursting into laughter.

Nurse of the year Mesude Hanım has given everyone a number and she is calling out names. The procedure falls apart after the fifth patient. Now she calls in whoever is closest to the door.

Toward noon the door opens and a dark, middle-aged man holding printouts from the population bureau comes in with a little girl. Clearly they have come for an age assessment report. Village teachers have the new students who have not been issued an ID card come into town to get one. The population bureau requires a report that assesses the age of the child based on bone development.

But of course we always ask the father for the age of his child:

"How old is she?"

Usually there is a pause before an answer:

"She's got some years on her. She must be six or nine or around there."

Now I know I'm not supposed to ask whether it's six or nine.

"Write it down, Mesude hanım ... The bone examination I have just done indicates the child is seven years old."

The man holds out the papers in empty space. Mesude hanım takes them and starts filling them out. I look at the child. Twisting behind her father, she is peering around the room. With those big eyes that look like black olives, she is an adorable, little girl.

"I am putting the age down as seven, Doctor," says Mesude hanım. I nod my head in approval.

"What's the child's name," says Mesude without looking up at the man.

Not a peep.

He just stands there as if the question wasn't addressed to him.

"I am asking you for the child's name. What is her name?"

Coming to his senses, he turns and looks at the girl and then at us. He looks back at the girl and stares for a while. Then with a strange smile on his face he turns, clears his throat, and says:

"*Valla* she hasn't got a name."

A silence falls over the room. Slightly surprised, I begin:

"How is that? You didn't give the child a name?"

He makes a strange gesture with his head that's impossible to decipher.

For a few moments we just stare at each other. But my curiosity doesn't let up:

"But then what do you call her? For example at home . . . what do you say?"

The man's face seems to light up for a moment:

"We call this one, dark girl. . . That's what we always call her. Dark girl."

"But she needs a name, no? To put on her ID."

The man doesn't say anything . . . For a while we just stand there like that. Blinking, the girl is frozen behind her father as if something truly undesirable is about to happen to her. Then with the pop of a motorbike engine out on the street, we all come to our senses.

"You give her a name, Doctor," says Mesude Hanım, worried.

I look at her face with a puzzled expression on mine. Yes, she means it.

"Fine then, alright. Let's give her a name . . . What shall it be?"

With a naïve smile on his face, the man listens to our conversation. It's all too clear that he feels like he has absolutely nothing to do with the matter.

Leaning back a little in my chair, I look out the window and over the endless steppes. I think of Brother Mehmet (Özgül), who came to visit dad with a copy of his own translations of Cengiz Aytmatov. It was the most beautiful gift of my childhood. For months I would lose myself in those beguiling stories about the steppes. Oh and there was Cemile.

"Let's call her Cemile," I say. It seems like the man hasn't even heard me. His little girl burrows a little deeper into his jacket as Mesude Hanım writes down the name Cemile on the blank space in the form.

★

I am in Istanbul. Working at a policlinic. A little after midnight. I am dozing off in an armchair when the front door slowly opens. Leading the way is our health officer Erdinç followed by two young men who are supporting a middle-aged woman between them. In the morbid light of the "Emergency" sign the procession leaves strange shadows in their wake as they slowly come over to me and stop. The woman is in an oddly forlorn state. Sitting her down on the examination table the two young men wait in silence. They are close in age, and clearly her children. One quickly takes a position over his mother and the other stands guard at the door: they seem worried about having forced her to come here and fear she might try to scramble out at the first opportunity.

I had to write down the woman's name and her condition in the policlinic log.

"Your name?" I ask.

There is a fleeting silence. The woman shifts on the table and mumbles something between her lips.

"Excuse me . . . I didn't catch that. What did you say?"

She has difficulty raising her voice.

"Duck."

The young man standing by the door lets out a grunt of laugh. The woman and the other man shoot daggers at him. But I am still not sure.

"Duck? So your name is Duck?"

Silently the woman confirms the name with a nod.

I forget about filling in the form and start the examination. The woman has chronic headaches and problems sleeping. But

I can't find an organic cause for her symptoms. Most of her complaints seem psychosomatic. I finish the examination still thinking about her name. I try getting her to talk by asking her all sorts of unrelated questions. Responding more and more she begins to open up and soon she seems much more at ease. Figuring now the time was right, I ask:

"So who gave you that name?"

"My dad, which he never should have done." Then she went on in a murmur:

"As if there was no other name."

"Why in the world would he choose a name like that?"

"He was really fond of ducks. That's what my mother used to say. So he gave me the name."

In a moment I go back all those years and that dark-haired, olive-eyed, nameless little girl comes to mind.

"I am going to change your name," I say, raising my voice slightly.

"Look, I am going to record your new name here in this book. And I am going to write you a prescription with your new name. I am giving you the name Cemile. From now everyone is going to call you that." Then turning to the young men:

"I have given your mother the name Cemile. From now on you are going to call her Mother Cemile, ok?"

They look at me in astonishment.

"When you run out of medicine and come back for a check up I want you to register with your new name, Cemile," I say, ending the conversation.

There is a twinkle in her eyes and her shoulders rise. She leaves the policlinic without her children under her arms.

A taxi drives down the deserted street outside. I hear the morning call to prayer from a distant mosque. Now I feel really tired and sleepy. Letting myself fall asleep in the arms of a country where all the sisters and mothers are called Cemile, I slowly close my eyes.

7
The Seal

Winter . . . I am in my third year at elementary school. We have moved out of the big house where we were living with our uncles and cousins and into a new house on the other side of the river. We are now what they call "cross-overs." There isn't much to the house but we are so happy all the same. Mom has draped her hand-woven carpets over the doors inside. My brother (two years older than me) and I have discovered how to bury potatoes in the ash that gathers at the bottom of our brand name "Eskişehir Sus" wood burning stove. We are waiting for him to come home. In my lap is Kemal Tahir's *Seven Plane Tree Meadow*, which I checked out of the Avanos Public Library. Last week our neighbor, who is a schoolteacher, came over to our house to visit dad during Eid:

"Mevlüt, who is reading this?"

"Our youngest son, hocam."

"This book is a little heavy for him. I don't think he should read it."

Dad doesn't say anything. In any event I'll be done with the book soon then start Jules Verne's *The Enchanted Island*.

Mom is collecting sacks of sugar she has washed over the stove and hung there to dry. A little later she puts several pans in front of me. These are gifts people brought to us before. One of them is unmarked and I write "Fadime of the Köse family." Carefully she wraps them up in newspaper. With a plastic bag filled with freshly washed sugar sacks in her other hand, she leaves the house.

38

I have fallen asleep with a book in my lap. Mom has been back for some time, and now she is standing over me. "Now get up and try these."

"What are those, mom?"

"Wool underwear, son. I had Sabiha Hanım sew them for you. Come try them on."

Aunt Sabiha graduated from the vocation school for girls. She is good with her hands. Mom asked her to make under-pants out of the sacks of sugar dad uses when he makes syrup for his soda. Happily I try on the underwear. They are nice but they seem a little rough and a bit of scratchy. But that's not a problem. Smack dab on the back is the brand name seal of the Kayseri Sugar Factory. Right out in the open. Which means it hasn't come out in the wash. I don't say anything about it to mom. Because she's so happy. But the label is there for all to see. What am I going to do when I have to change in front of everyone in gym class? I spent two years changing in the bath-room before class because of the sugar label on those shorts mom had Aunt Sabiha make for me...

★

During my years of mandatory civil service, I became familiar with the judiciary seal.

A nine or ten years old child is silently sitting across from me. Mentally disabled from birth. There is a gendarmerie officer beside me. A little further on is the boy's father lost in thought, his head bowed. The gendarmerie hands me the report. "Anal intercourse." It was the boy's uncle. The official report itself is a disaster. When they took down statements they made a real mess of everything. All these strange questions and needless details. They asked and came to their own conclusions.

Have you ever felt ashamed for simply sharing the same world with someone? This was one of those times.

I look at the boy. He hardly knows what has happened to him. What's troubling him is the purple justice department seal on the inside of his wrist. Now and then he looks at it and at one point I see he is trying to rub it off. Slowly he brings the seal to his lips, spits and tries to wipe it off. The gendarmerie nudges the boy in the shoulder:

"Don't rub it off."

Helpless, the boy stops. I call over the nurse:

"Bring me a cloth with some alcohol on it. Let's rub this off your wrist."

The gendarmerie grows nervous and objects.

"I will speak with your commanding officer. You don't need to worry about it."

A little later a faint smile takes shape on the boys face. What did I do? That smile was probably one of the best gifts I received in all my days.

★

About a year has passed since the coup. I am at school in Izmir. Not out in public very much. Now I can't remember if there was an incident or if it was just that my name was bandied about when dad calls me from Avanos.

"You need to come and give a statement," he says.

I went to the police station that looks nothing like it did before the coup; no trace of those words "Down with Fascism" written on the wall; it seemed as if this new massive structure had pushed out the old one. It was that imposing . . . Anyway. The chief inspector looks at my ID. He knows me. The picture on my card is of an innocent, clean-faced kid just out of High School. "How did you change so much?" he says.

His voice carries that sarcastic tone that comes with power. Of course he has every right, in the end they are going to read us the riot act. "Well I did grow a mustache," I say.

How should I put it now? He pauses for a moment. Am I being serious or horsing around? "I'm not asking about your moustache, son. I'm asking about what's up there in your head. Has your thinking changed?"

"No," I say. "Same as always. Just like it was before."

He looks upset but doesn't raise his voice. That evening in the club he tells everybody about it. Later dad is in a foul mood under the vine outside our house, telling his "story of the seal," which I would hear again and again:

"You know Ilhan Abi. When he was a student at university he went to a meyhane one day with his friends. While they are singing all the folk songs one of them decides to read a poem by Nazım Hikmet. Someone goes and informs the police, saying he was 'peddling communist propaganda.' So the police round them all up and take them away. As they were doing background checks and taking statements it turns out that the inspector was from Avanos. Luckily he didn't book them. He let them all go. But he gave them a piece of his mind. He said: 'Son, in this country they mark goat as lamb and sell it on the streets. You can struggle all you want and say you are a goat. But you have already been labeled a lamb. And that's what you will always be.' If they label you a 'communist' you keep the label for the rest of your life. So hurry up and get out of here."

I am overseeing the building of a hospital in Istanbul. Dad is watching me with apprehension. He keeps going on about why I resigned from my management position in the state hospital and got wrapped up in something like this when I'm broke. At last the hospital is finished and dad has come from Avanos and I'm showing him around. The operating room, patients' rooms, the morgue, everything. Clearly he is proud of me. In my office we have coffee.

"Give the hospital an official seal, son. You can't not have one," he says.

I later lost my dad in my own hospital. That night I put him in the morgue he had once praised. After living out a pure and meaningful life he was brought back to the steppes where he would be laid to rest at the foot of his mother's grave with the seal of the hospital on the report for the burial of the deceased.

★

Turkey in the wake of the 1980 September 12 coup will be remembered as a time when families searched for their sons who had gone missing. It was the middle of the night when the police arrived at the home of Ramazan Yukarıgöz, who had been executed during the 1983 junta. The body of the young man was now sealed in a coffin. Here is how his mother describes that night:

"Someone was banging on the door in the middle of the night. I got up straightaway. It was the police."

"What's wrong? What's happened?" I said.

"Is this Ramazan's house?" they said.

"What happened? Did something happen to Ramazan?" I said. I woke up his father. He went out to speak with them next to their car.

"Where do you want to have him buried? Are you going to have a funeral or not?" they asked. His father started pounding the car with his fist.

"Of course we are going to arrange for his funeral. If they are going to take away the living then we will take away the dead. What do you mean, not have his funeral?" he said. That's when I fell to the floor...

"I want to see my child," I said.

"You can't," they said.

"Why not?" I asked and they told me:

"The coffin is sealed shut."

"Your seal means nothing for me," I said and I pushed them aside and I tore it off. I opened the coffin. It looked as if his hair had been freshly combed. His eyebrows were perfectly straight. He was beautiful in a completely different way. I kissed his face..."

★

In composition class our high school literature teacher Zafer Bey had us write some juicy stuff. I was first in my class but I used to sit in the back row with the troublemakers. During free periods we would go down to the stream behind the school to secretly drink vodka and listen to Ferdi Tayfur. The source of my angst was a green-eyed girl I couldn't open up to. Zafer Hoca would come to me in the back row, pull a little bottle of cologne from his pocket, tap a few drops onto his palm and inhale the vapors briefly as he said:

"*Sevda* is a dark seal. For those in the grip of the dark passion most certainly have this seal on their hearts."

I have performed countless autopsies. And I have assisted in just as many. Whenever I put my scalpel over a heart, my eyes search for that dark seal. I wonder if what Zafer Hoca said was true. Do we have such a thing on our hearts?

For some ridiculous reason one of the rooms in the policlinic where I was working was officially sealed. I asked the health officer, who went crazy with fear every time an officially sealed envelope arrived, about this particular seal:

"What will happen if we break it?"

"Oh dear, hocam, you are talking about a 'breach of the seal.' Such a thing simply isn't done."

"But I mean, what will actually happen?"

"I don't know."

"Well let's break it then. . ."

Don't you think the time for us to break the seals around our hearts has long since come?

8
Whose Blood Is That on the Photo?

An August evening. A sweet coolness in the air. Blowing fire out of every nook and cranny throughout the day, the steppes are finally settling down for a cold evening. Now is when you might shiver to the bone if you don't throw something over your shoulders. Shopkeepers have long since shuttered their shops. Only the coffeehouses and the Civil Servants' club are still open. A regular in the club, Mithat is wearing a dirty undershirt and waving about a plastic bag as he excitedly tells something to baker Halil, who is sitting in a chair in front of the oven with his legs crossed. It is perfectly clear he isn't paying attention to Mithat. One of the village minibuses is running late, the driver busy shoving an oversized sofa bed into the back. A harvester sways from side to side as it slowly turns onto a dirt road that winds up into the fields. For him the day has just begun, he will reap until morning.

When I first heard the sound I was in the kitchen cracking an egg. Earlier that evening I was struggling to bring down the temperature of a little boy who had been transferred to the health clinic. In the late hours of the evening his fever finally fell and he seemed somewhat relieved. I hurried off to make something to eat. I was in the kitchen of my bachelor's residence next to the hospital when I heard that strange cracking. It sounded like a harsh rap on a piece of wood or a little like the popping of one of those cork guns we used to fire during religious holidays. Three or four shots one after the other. I went out onto the balcony and had a good look around. The shots had come from the gas station a little further on from the hospital. I could just barely make out a station wagon speeding down a dirt road. After a moment of silence people dashed over to the station and formed a crowd.

I knew that I would be called over soon so I quickly finished my eggs.

By the time I got there the man was long since dead. A dark, fairly stout, middle-aged man. He was from out of town. Otherwise I would have recognized him. He looked like a farmer from one of the surrounding villages. One of his tractor tires had burst and he had come to the station to have it repaired. His tractor was still up on the hoist, suspended in mid air. When the farmer saw the killer he must have fled to the toilet but didn't make it. Lying face down on the ground, he was wearing only one shoe. The other had flown off his foot. Blood that had gushed out of the back of his head was already beginning to dry. Bullet holes were clearly marked on the back of his shirt. An inner tube was gently undulating in an old bucket of water next to an air pump. The dead man had found the rupture and had stuck a broken match into the hole. That broken match in a tractor inner tube was the strange, forlorn sign of an unfinished job.

An hour later I was checking the body of the deceased into the hospital morgue. A police office was filling a bag with the man's personal effects when I asked if I could have a look at the ID. The card was smeared in blood and because the corner of its plastic casing was slightly chipped a photograph slipped out and fell onto the table. It was a portrait of a little girl looking shyly through her dark, braided hair. She was dressed in a black pinafore and a white shirt. It was clearly a photo taken at her primary school registration. So her dad kept a copy in his wallet. Now the little girl must be out on the street, racing about with her friends, letting out whoops of joy, before she had to go home. Or she is already fast asleep, her beautiful head on her poor mother's knees. She still doesn't know that she is a fatherless child.

*

On my first day in the dorm in Bornova I put a small poster of Sezen Aksu (the kind they gave away with cassette albums) on the door of my metal locker, the ones assigned to every student. "The Little Swallow." Perched on the edge of a chair, Sezen Aksu is trying to strike a sexy pose with her big lips and a playful look in her eyes; but in every pose she always gives off a childlike innocence. In those days it was my only poster that survived as the gendarmerie were always raiding the dorms and ripping everything out of our lockers. By then I had given up on looking for another poster of Che Guevara because he was ripped out every time.

Some time later I put up a photograph next to the picture of Sezen Aksu, one I had torn out of a magazine in the French Cultural Center. E. Smith's photograph "A Country Doctor." I carried that photograph around with me for years. Like it was my fate. After I finished school and went to the Keskin State hospital to start my mandatory civil service that photograph loomed over the head of my bed in the free hospital room where I was living at the time. Twenty-five years later when we went back to some of the same places to shoot a movie we put the exact same photograph on the doctor's wall. During the shoot, colleagues, staff members and my driver Gara Gazi from 25 years ago all came to visit me. They showed me the old photographs they kept in their wallets. Most of them were pictures of friends who were no longer alive. There was a picture of Arif the photographer, Split Yaşar, Brother Mevlüt the Head Surgeon, and Heavy Crimes Brother Reisi Hamit. Together, after so many years, we looked at those photographs but more than that we looked back over our shared lives. A sense of destiny had seeped into them.

★

Dad never failed to arrange photographs he felt were important along the frame of the mirror in the living room. As my cousins grew there were more and more pictures. At first there were more pictures of me that lined the edge of the mirror but soon those were replaced by pictures of my cousins' weddings and their newborn babies. Whenever dad came to Istanbul and needed to buy anything he would immediately hand me his wallet and say, "son, there's a card in here and the password is written on a slip of paper beside it. Take out as much as we need." Unable to tell him that I had more money than everything he had in his modest pensioner's account, I would quietly take his wallet. While I pretended to locate his card and its password, I would have a good look around. Next to his ID card are five or six business cards he must have felt were the important ones, a newspaper clipping "A Cure for Parkinson's is Discovered," a picture of me and my moustache when I was registering as a student in the Politics Department, and tucked away inside is a little portrait of my niece who died when she was very young . . .

That's how it is. Some photographs hit you right in the heart and the same way every time.

Here is what a photographer friend of mine who was lucky enough to make it out of the fire in Sivas said about what happened:

"I say to myself I am going to die. There's no way out of here. The people out there are going to burn us alive. So at least I should try to save the photos I took in the hotel. I pulled out the film and slipped it into an envelope. I put that in my wallet and then pressed that against my body. I was thinking that when they found my body they would definitely find those photographs . . ."

And so we have those burnt, pungent photos of brothers Metin and Behçet sitting in desperation on the stairs of the Madımak Hotel. Photographs that were pressed closely to the body of my friend.

★

Photographs can sometimes bring unexpected surprises. Open up doors you never would have thought of. My wife was acting in a film when she recommended me to the director for a minor role. He said, "what's he look like?" and she showed him the picture of me she always kept in her wallet. Maybe my adventure as a cinema actor began the moment he said those words, "ok then, let's go with him."

The story of Naile is another story altogether. One evening Naile was killed by two people whose photographs she carried in her purse. Naile was 16 when she was raped but no one in her family knew about her pregnancy. When she went to hospital with an unrelated complaint her condition became apparent. Doctors surmised what had happened to her and they detained her. A prosecutor was apprised of the situation. Naile's father then promised the prosecutor they would come for Naile and her baby four days after the birth. Indeed they came and fetched her from the hospital but that same night Naile's older brother told her he was going to take her out for a walk and they left the house together. Her mother encouraged her to go. And right there in the middle of the street her brother shot her dead. In her purse she always carried the photographs of her father and her brother: photographs of the people who had killed her. Naile's blood was on them.

The story of Cyrano comes to mind. You know how Roxanne struggles to understand why he didn't tell her that he had written the letters himself. Remembering his fiancée who had died in the war, Cyrano answers: "The words are mine but the blood on them is hers."

What difference does it make if everything we write is indeed our own. But the blood on the words, and the unfortunate stories that we indifferently listen to every day . . . This is what we must know . . .

9

The Smell of Bread or Blood?

Just at the entrance to the garden in front of his house is a black oven up against a wall. Tile Maker Hacı Amca built it. I remember it so well, the way he slowly worked at it as if doing nothing at all. With bands on her arms, mom is making cheese and potato flatbread with lean beef. My ebe Cemelli's face is turned to the sun; I'm wearing my argyle sweater; my brother is sitting on a leather stool he made himself. I am with my ebe. Now she is quite old and her memory isn't all that good. Every now and then someone passes by the house with a hoe or a shovel on his shoulder. These are seasonal laborers who have come from Sarıhıdır, Bayramhacılı and Kışlalı. Quickly my ebe raises her stick and points them out to mom: "Fadime ... Look, he's almost gone, call him over. Come on, come on ..." Without even answering, mom hurriedly wraps one or two of the flatbreads stacked to one side in a newspaper and barely catches up to the passing laborer. Every time she comes back she looks down at the mounds of dough on the ground and mumbles to herself. The flatbread is going to run out. But my ebe is all too pleased with herself.

"All these people are all alone, my lamb. They aren't married and they don't have a home. Now they surely picked up the scent of the fresh bread. Who is going to make food for them? What will they eat and drink ... Only good deeds."

I grew up in a house where everyone hurried to hand out food to a beggar who had come to the door so that the good deed might go down in the books. In all her 90 years my ebe knew nothing of the world outside our home and

Kızılöz—indeed she had never seen the world outside our home and Kızılöz—but in my heart of hearts she was the wisest woman in the world. And then she got Alzheimer's. She was always asking us about the past and whenever she came to an open door she wanted to hurry back to Cemel. When mom could no longer handle the situation, I would come out with a performance. Dressed in dad's coat and a with village cap on my head, I was transformed into a relative who had come from Cemel on a visit.

"Mother Cemelli, I am here. From Cemel . . . Ibraam."

"Oh my lamb! Ibraam has come. Fadime, look who has come to visit! Welcome my lamb."

Mom knew the conversation could go on for a while so she used to go out to the back garden. Taking my ebe by the hands, I would set out an exciting adventure through her lost world I knew nothing about, drawing on the intuition of a child. My ebe was married to Mustafa of the Köse family and so of course she would ask after his fields, his sheep and his lambs and his wheat in the fields and tell me to pass on her regards to all her relatives. Some time later she would kiss my hands and, filled with greetings for everyone in Cemel, I would leave the house, setting the jacket and hat beside the pool where they would wait for me until my next visit. It made my ebe so happy.

"Oh Fadime, will you just look at that, girl. The wheat is doing really well this year. God praise, God praise! Oh let it be good, and may God not punish people with hunger."

My ebe left me with a pure innocence, an endless drive and the smell of bread that prompted the hunger of people she didn't know.

★

My university years. A time when we were always hungry. We had been thrown out of the dorm. I had a tough correspondence with dad. I had made myself clear in the harshest terms.

"I don't want your money so don't send any!"

For a while I was going to the hired hand meeting point in Karşıyaka. I was playing the part of the wild young man who couldn't go to university after high school and who couldn't find a job. I was working on a stud farm construction site in Şemikler with Kurdish laborers. When we broke for lunch we all went to a working class restaurant. A small helping of beans, a little rice and loads of bread. The only thing all those workers crowded around a wooden table would say was:

"Brother, more bread . . ."

In Bornova I generally go to the coffeehouse across from the hospital. I am flat broke. In a corner sits a thin, gaunt, sallow-faced man. He is one of the negative group blood donors. These people are selling their own blood. Every now and then the door to the coffeehouse swings open and a hurried voice says, "O Rh negative." Someone from the group stands up and after a brief conversation they all leave together. What these donors most want from med students are sample blood stimulators and iron supplement pills. They call them-selves "döner" (as in the Turkish kebab), inspired by the word donor in English, as if referring to something that slims down as it's sliced. Tactfully I ask them how much they get for a bottle of blood. Not bad, it's actually good money, enough to get by on. So I go to Kızılay to sell some of my blood. In the evening I go to a friend's dilapidated house in Alsancak with a load of supplies. I have eggs, bread, a little ground beef and halvah. And there's always plenty of tea and cigarettes. Seven or eight of us have founded a folklore group at the university, and everyone here is hungry and expecting me at the house. All the dancers are leftists but the drummer Mehmet has nothing to do with all that. As I prepare the food I talk to him about socialism and that sort of stuff. You see I'm trying to enlighten them. Going on about added value and dialectics and the fate of the country. It doesn't seem to be sinking in with Mehmet but he keeps quiet. Then we sit down around a low table. Eight people huddled around a big tray. Without noticing it I push the eggs that had come round to me out to the center. Toward the end of the meal Mehmet says in a quiet voice:

"Brother Ercan, now I understand socialism. Now I know who these people are, the people they call socialists. A socialist is someone who offers his eggs to his friends even when he's hungry."

★

I am in Istanbul. Now I am running the hospital. I no longer have hunger issues but I have brothers in the hospital who do. The long hunger strikes that began in 2000 have come to an end and the strikers who are still alive have started their recovery. Several have come to my hospital. But no one quite knows just what kind of treatment is needed. This is the longest hunger strike in recorded history. These young men are nothing but skin and bones, stuck in their beds, and the silken hair of the women has become so fine it's hardly even there. Looking out at the world through faded eyes from an eerie darkness, they are lost in a blurred consciousness, unaware that the strike is over.

I was under the impression the days when people lay down to die from hunger to teach others were over. I was wrong. It seems that's not the case. That's just the way it is. Oppression and hostility never went away. How quickly I forgot the story of Cain and Abel. The marble altars await new victims. Come on, let's all gather round and idly watch. But notice how small it is. We can't all fit around the table of this earth. We are drowning in a sea of pride and we have no idea that our mills have fallen silent and our flour is gone. Our ovens have turned black like our hearts.

Now it is not the smell of bread in the air but the smell of blood . . .

Alright then. What should we say? Bon apetit . . .

10
What's Left for Us

"Yaşar Bey and his friend from the Bülbül Neighborhood are waiting outside. They would like to see you," said my secretary and I hesitated for a moment. Bülbül is a neighborhood below Dolapdere, on the way up to Taksim. I couldn't recall a Yaşar Bey. But so be it. "Have them come in."

A little later a short, middle-aged man who was lame in one foot and dressed in a shabby black suit came into my office with a chubby-faced, young man. Yaşar Bey and his friend. With a grateful expression on his face, Yaşar began:

"How do you do, Doctor? Yaşar, from Bülbül. Do you remember me? This here is my friend Kamil." I didn't and so naturally I said:

"Of course, Yaşar Bey, please.".

"The girl's fine now ... Last Sunday our friends looked after her, many thanks to them. You called and warned them. About the money. Her fever broke. We had the tests again and she was fine. So you see, for the last couple days me and Kamil have been knocking our heads together, wondering what we could do for the doctor. We heard you liked the clarinet. So in the end we decided on that."

Turning to the large man who was quietly listening, Yaşar said:

"Come on then, Kamil."

Opening up a box that he had tucked under his chair, Kamil pulled out a clarinet. He slowly put the pieces together. He wet the reed. Blew a couple times. Then he began a graceful

54

improvisation. My friend the dentist who happened to be there with me in my office and who was watching everything in astonishment got up and firmly shut the door behind him. A little later the mournful sound of the clarinet was echoing through the hospital as patients in the waiting room tilted their heads, trying to locate the source of the music.

After a while Yaşar gently tapped Kamil. The music stopped. The clarinet was carefully put away in its box. Yaşar said:

"Doctor we could never pay you enough, we're musicians, and so this is all that we have to offer you. Nothing more. So please accept this." They left in silence, as if they had never come.

We were in each other's lives. Whether we wanted to be or not.

How can you disregard the story of a retiree from Erzincan with a failing liver and a house condemned to destruction because of urban development? Or the case of an ambitious young footballer who is wild about sports and who had a lump removed from his leg that may or may not be malignant, his father a laborer from Alucra who was fired from his job the day before. Wouldn't you worry about it? Could you just examine a mother from Tunceli, write a prescription for her rheumatism and send her home when you know that she lost one of her sons to a long hunger strike while the other son languishes in prison? Wouldn't you ask her more? How else could you be truly "altruistic?"

★

Izmir ... In those days when we all feel the full weight of the 1980 military coup. They have detained one of my dearest friends from med school and we have no idea what's happened to him or where he is. His brother-in-law comes and asks for my advice.

"What are we going to do? No word from him for the last five days. Where could he be?"

I have already come to fear my own shadow. Nevertheless I try to come up with a plan. The next day his brother-in-law gets word that our friend is being held in the infamous political branch of the security building in Konak. He comes to the school cafeteria and says, "let's go over together." Having a fairly good idea of what might happen to me, I trudge over to the political branch with my friend's brother-in-law. We ask after our friend:

"Is he here, is he OK?"

Just imagine the setting and how we go about it: there we are asking a wolf about a lamb. They rough up the brother-in-law a little and send him on his way but at the last minute they decide to detain me. We are 30 people packed into a 10-meter-square cell. Waiting for whatever it is that is going to happen next. In a room that is always dark you eventually lose your sense of time. But the set meals they slip under the door give us some sense of the time of day. In the morning it's soup and in the evening dried beans or rice. Truth is I don't take what's happened to me too seriously. Something like this would strike me as a disaster now but in those days it was somehow just put down as run-of-the mill. But how wonderful those days were. Anyway. So there I am still worried about my friend. He must be in one of the neighboring cells. "What's he doing right now? Is he all right? Have they tortured him? How is he holding up?" That's what's running through my mind. I think it was the fifth day when they gave us a mushy *kadayıf* with the meal. *Tel Kadayıf*. Unbelievable. It's our friend's favorite dessert. I know how crazy he is about it. And in that moment it seemed like everything disappeared: the September 12 coup, politics, fascism, everything. The idea of my friend eating *Tel kadayıf* right then was everything and the rest didn't mean a thing. Now everything was beautiful.

We were in each other's lives. Even if we had no idea.

★

My late granddad on mom's side was a butcher. I always remember how he used to spot me when I was downtown distributing soda and he would call me over, take a piece of bread out of his classic handkerchief and, filling it with meat (he always made these delicious stews and homemade *kuşgönü* pastrami), he would stuff it into my mouth. I would see him in the afternoon when I managed to get away from my brothers and the *gazozhane* and make for town. There he was sitting absentmindedly on one of the benches near the mosque, leaning on his cane. When he saw me his eyes would light up and he would call me over right away:

"Are you hungry, my lamb?"

From the tone in his voice I know how wholeheartedly he wants me to be hungry. So even when I'm full I won't let on. I know his tasty rice made in those little copper pots and those sausages dangling from the ceiling in his cellar under a cool rock and his fragrant butter from his little fridge are all waiting for me. As I eat granddad sits opposite me and watches.

I learned from granddad that "being human" means passing on to others those things that make you happy. You are human when you want for others the same things you want for yourself, and just as badly.

We are in each other's lives and I imagine that being human possibly means more than just altruism.

When I was a child and delicious or remarkable dishes were on the table, mom would immediately begin saying: "Oh my, bring a slice of this to your aunt Fetiye," or "don't finish that, leave some for your uncle Muharrem." Despite dad's subtle teasing, mom would carry on in the same way: "Karoğlan would love this so leave a plate for him. And I have already set aside a leg for uncle Memiş so take that over to him before it gets cold."

Are you aware that whenever you put something delicious in your mouth the first thing that comes to mind tells you who you are?

★

Dad is now bedridden and in the late stages of Parkinson's. Mom was kneeling down to pray beside him when she noticed he wasn't making a sound. "I said hello … 'Mevlüt,' I said, 'Mevlüt.' No answer. I went over to him. Took his hands, they were cold. So be it, they are always cold … But his mouth was clenched. No breath. That's when I knew. Then I remembered you were eating *mantı*. I went to the door and I called the nurse. Don't tell my son. Let him finish his *mantı* first, then tell him. He's crazy about his dad, he'll come running, and he won't finish eating."

When you see your friend gently crying when you tell him the story of how your mother quietly waited beside your late father so that you could finish eating; or when you take a bite of food and realize you can't swallow; or if you feel the need to breathe in the scent of your son in a country where mothers are burying their sons one after the other then you have begun to notice the lives of others. And that's also a good thing. For now . . .

11
A Drop of Water

The endlessly falling snow had covered the entire town in a warm and loving blanket. Where the high steps of the public library meet the street I have my back against the wall, waiting for the library to open. A little later the old concierge Yaşar Efendi walks past me and starts climbing the steps. I can feel him looking at me out of the corner of his eye. The scrawny kid waiting at the library steps! Trailing two or three steps behind him, I am careful to keep the same pace. After dawdling on the doorstep, he unlocks the door with a massive key. He gives his shoes a good cleaning on the grated metal mat in front of the double-winged wooden door. The thing is I know all too well that he's doing it just because I am there. Then he goes inside and stands beside the door. I rub my old wet shoes back and forth over the mat. In silence and with an unchanging expression on his face, he watches me. After staring for a while he must think I've rubbed enough because he disappears inside. Now I can go in. There's no one else there. I go and sit down at the table by a window. I am half way through *The Enchanted Island* and my plan is to pick up where I left off. Taking the book off the shelf, I make for the table where the registration book is. Holding a bucket of coal beside the stove, Yaşar Efendi watches me. He's searching for a reason to be angry with me but I haven't made a mistake yet. I have done everything precisely the way he wants it to be done. I go over to my spot and oh, now that's more like it. As I pull out the heavy chair, there is an unwanted squeak. Flashing me a reproachful look and shaking his head, Yaşar dumps coal into the stove. So be it, now I am reunited with my book. Soon the library warms up and the room is filled with noisy children shivering from the cold. A coughing, laughing, jostling crowd. They are all my friends. Swimming in their old jackets and stumbling about in their weak, little bodies, the kids plop down in the first chair they find and start to take in the surroundings. There is a swirling hum in the air that smells of shoes and wet socks. People come and go, open the door to look inside then disappear and the squeaking of the chairs picks up. Overwhelmed by the rising noise and jostling crowd, Yaşar Efendi momentarily disappears through a door to a small room off the main room. When the door opens with a squeak the ancient head librarian, Mehmet Bey, is standing there on the threshold.

He would then begin with the same line he used every time, which I will never forget, emphasizing every word and with the same tone of voice:

"You fill a glass with water. Fill it but it doesn't overflow. Fill it to the brim and still it does not overflow. But one more drop and it does. Just one drop. Do you know what? One more drop and this glass overflows!"

★

The old man with a chubby red face has been lying in the internal medicine ward for a week. He is overweight but he has a beautiful, supple body. And he has high blood pressure, a weak heart. His rather tall, dark wife with a pockmarked face is looking after him. The patient gets on well with me and the nurses. The other night he had chest pains and I stayed by his side till morning not sleeping a wink, and he was very grateful. I know that his eyes light up when he sees me. He knows that I'm single so he's become a matchmaker, choosing according to his own tastes the best looking nurse working the shift. As she comes and goes he tries to convince me. The nurses giggle whenever he gets talking. With a strange smile on her face, the man's wife silently observes his childish behavior.

When the nurse called for me I was writing a letter to dad. I raced over. The old man has been vomiting excessively and he is disoriented. Is there hemorrhaging in his stomach? Trying to determine the source of the problem, I noticed a strong smell of garlic in the room and his wife who is reading the Koran as if nothing is wrong.

While I examine the patient I quietly pray for the internist to come quickly. Why would this suddenly happen to a patient we have under such close observation? Before I can ask the nurse says:

"Sir, I was going to tell you before but I didn't have the chance. This morning I caught his relatives feeding him a handful of garlic. To bring his blood pressure down more quickly. I think they have been feeding him handful after handful of garlic for the last three or four days."

Just then the old man stops breathing and his heart goes out. We are losing him. Quickly I begin heart resuscitation, trying to clear some space on the bed as I start the procedure. In the middle of all the commotion the man's wife is the only one in the room who looks as if nothing is wrong. Struggling to bring the man back to life, I feel her slowly take my hand. For a moment we come eye to eye. I look at her and she says:

"Stop, my son. Don't torment the man. His glass is full. His life is done. He wanted a drop and you can see it has fallen. So don't try."

We lost the old man. Not from high blood pressure or a weak heart, but from the bleeding in his stomach.

★

It was the day of a religious holiday. I got up early to kiss mom and dad's hands before retreating to a corner. From the living estate garden came the sounds of bustling children. Dressed in jackets that are clearly part of special outfits for the holiday, residents of the estate pass by our window on their way to visit neighbors. Mom's lips are fluttering in quick pursuit of who knows what prayer. Dad keeps saying that his medicine makes him itch.

"What if we dropped them altogether, son? And I don't take them at all?" he said, frustrated. I paused for a moment and said:

"Ok dad, let's drop them, stop taking them."

He gave me such a look. I knew that he knew I was angry.

"Dad, you know you can't not take your medicine," I said, softening my voice.

Gazing hopelessly out the window, he began speaking of Semih Bey, his commander in the army:

"One day they said, 'there is going to be shooting practice; and the people who hit the target will be rewarded leave time.' So of course everyone got really into the idea. On our way to the shooting range Semih Bey kicked my foot and said, 'Shoot wide, shoot wide.' I didn't understand what he was saying but I kept shooting for the trailer. But of course the Kurds always turned out to be the best shooters. It's still the same. They sent all the top shooters out to hunt the mountain men in the east. Waiting to set out on their 'reward leave' those soldiers cried to think they were being sent out to kill their own brothers. 'For the love of God, commander, kill us before you send us there.' Then they all got their dog tags." There was sadness in dad's voice.

A strange silence fell over the room. Truth is I was in a bad mood.

"Dad, where is Semih Bey now?" I asked.

"I think he was in Mersin," he said, wrestling his wallet out of his inside jacket pocket. I know that in these moments I have to help him. I took his wallet and we started to spread out the business cards he kept beside the bank card he used to withdraw his pension. Yes, here it is, Semih Bey's business card. Years ago on a trip to Mersin he managed to track down his commander and after a chat he took his business card.

"I can get in touch with him if you want?" I said.

"Really? Is that possible?" he said and then waited in silence. With the number on the card and using a missing number service, I reached the commander's daughter.

"My dad died two years ago," she said. At first I didn't say anything and then I asked her for her mother's number. A little later I had the commander's wife on the line. I carried the phone to dad who was sitting in an armchair. Trembling, he rose to his feet, my 85-year-old dad with Parkinsons.

"Yes it's me, Mevlüt."

I turned up the volume. This woman was clearly younger than dad but she addressed him as "my son Mevlüt." Dad was shaken to get the news of Semih Bey's passing.

"Is that so? We have lost the commander? Is that so?" he said a couple times.

"How are you, my son? How is your health?" Semih Bey's wife asked.

Then dad repeated those words with a resolve that startled me every time I heard them:

"I am fine, madam. Just old age. The glass is full, just one drop to go. Waiting for it to fall, madam."

12
Just Let Go

"Hurry up and drink this."

Mom was standing over me with a glass of water.

"What's that, mom? I didn't ask for water."

"Drink it up, sweetie. Nimet Abla drank the first half, now you drink the rest."

"Why?"

"Don't ask why. Just drink it so you get some of her in you. Come on, drink."

Nimet Abla was one of the village girls who had gone to university. Her mom came to help mine with chores; day and night they would weave carpets. Mom was a fan of Nimet Abla. "She's a really smart girl," she said whenever she saw her. This meant every time she came over mom would have her drink half a glass of water and save the second half for me. I finished my half and went to bed. In the morning I was going to Istanbul to take the entrance exams at the Kuleli Military High School. Mom got everything ready before we left: a talisman with a powerful prayer in my coat pocket, holy grains of rice in the secret pocket in my bag and this half a glass of water.

We traveled to Istanbul where I failed the physical education exam. I was last place in the race and I couldn't do any of the calisthenics. I remember the sad look on my dad's face as I struggled to do a pull-up, my arms too weak to lift my body over the bar even once.

It was July. Istanbul was beautiful. As beautiful as those first scoops of ice-cream I'd eaten out of a glass bowl.

Dad disappeared and came back with bathing suits.

On the coast and in the middle of the crowd, we changed with towels wrapped around our waists. I was looking at the sea for the first time and I was going to swim in it. Clutching the edge of the pier, I slowly lowered myself into the water. But I couldn't let go.

"Slowly kick your feet," dad said. "The water will keep you afloat."

I thought of the Kızılırmak River and how you had to thrash about and use your arms to swim. But that was nothing like the sea. How wonderful is the sea, the way the water lifts you up. But I still couldn't let go. Dad leaned over and softly said:

"Don't be scared, son . . . Just let go."

I looked into his eyes. Yes, I could do it. Slowly I released my grip on the pier and started to swim.

★

I'm in my first few months of mandatory service. In a town on the steppes of Anatolia. A 24-year-old kid in the middle of nowhere.

There are no rooms left in the boarding house and a long waiting line to get in. So they put me in an empty room in the hospital. Just an old bunk, an unused medicine cabinet and a Formica table. All I need. The central heating's running all the time and I'm never cold. Several times a week I go to the hamam across from the hospital. The girl at the main post office likes me because I don't make her wait for her mother-in-law's prescriptions; my "standard" telephone calls are connected as "lightning" calls. All's well in the world.

I spend my nights in the hospital so naturally I am always on call. The nurses wake me up first. Every time I go to see a patient in the emergency room my heart is pounding in my chest. First I examine the patient. Silently I ask myself all the questions, trying to arrange them in my mind.

Then the same act: "Nurse, take the patient's blood pressure again and check his temperature." I calmly open the door, step into the corridor as if I am heading to the bathroom and then

I dive into my room. Thick medical books are resting on the table in the middle of the room, some open, some stuffed with notes. I rifle through them in a panic.

With scrap notes in my pocket and the names of the right medicine in my head, I go back to see the patient, drying my hands as if I had just come out of the bathroom.

It is a cold winter day. Midnight. A north wind swirling around all corners. All the other doctors are on extended leave for the holiday. I'm the only one in the hospital. They pull me out of a deep sleep. The patient was brought to the hospital in a tractor from a faraway village. He's a middle-aged man, fat and olive-skinned, and he can't urinate. As if guilty of a crime, he says, squirming:

"Doctor, forgive me but I've been a wreck for the last three days. Pardon me for saying this, but I can't pee . . ." After examining him, I decide to give him a catheter. The patient's willing to try anything as long as he's relieved of the pain. I ask him to lie down and then I nervously insert the catheter. No urine. Did I put it in the wrong way? Now I'm dripping in sweat.

But it really isn't all that bad. Handan is the nurse on duty. I have a soft spot for her.

I look at her as if to say, "what do we do now?" The patient is still moaning, "Oh God, just do something, doctor." For this kind of condition there is only one other option. I've seen the procedure once during my internship, but I've never done it myself. Insert a needle through the lower abdomen and into the bladder and then drain the urine.

I decide to go for it. I ask the patient to lie down and check the precise location of his bladder before I apply a local anesthetic, then I slowly insert the tube from top to bottom. I have a tight grip on it—I can't let go. My heart is racing. What if I puncture his intestines or another organ? Minutes seem to last forever. Nothing. No urine. Oh my God. What do I do know? Then Handan says in a gentle voice:

"Doctor, just let go. Don't worry."

I look at her face. She leans closer, whispering:

"Don't worry. Just let go."

The tube has entered the patient's bladder but I am holding onto it so tightly I am obstructing the passage. I let go. Seconds later urine begins to flow and the patient lets out a deep sigh.

★

Dad is lying on the old sofa bed in the sunroom of the entrance to our house. I'm sitting on a plastic chair watching him. We stay like that for some time in silence. All of a sudden I hear the sound of water in the garden. Mom must have turned on the electric pump. Struggling, he pulls his leg up to his stomach. Then he picks up a stained napkin from the corner of the sofa and wipes his lips. Mom is coming and going with a tray, mumbling to herself. The popping of a scooter engine fades away at the end of the road and is gone. I'm thinking of going downtown. I could have a stroll, buy a few newspapers, maybe have a tea with an old friend. I'm looking for a good excuse to get up and go. I stir in my seat. He's watching me, too.

"Take me to Kızılöz," he says. I pause for a moment.

"Now, dad?"

Without answering me, he says:

"I haven't been in such a long time. I'm wondering what it's like now."

I feel a little trapped. I was about to go downtown.

"Alright, dad. Come on then, get up and I'll take you there."

Half an hour later we're in Kızılöz. Where he grew up. We see all the little houses, stables and rooftops he worked on when he was a hired hand. Most of them are in ruins, farm animals kept in what remains. Several stray dogs wander through the rubble. I carefully help dad out of the car. The summer is over, the season sliding into fall. A wind blows off the steppes and we shiver. Leaning on his cane, dad looks around. I can tell he's looking for our old home. He starts walking toward one of the crumbled homes on a hilltop. Now he's full of life and energy, healthy again. Silently I follow him. He arrives at a broken wall and gazes out over the hills like he has spotted something. I step over to him and stand beside him in silence. For a moment his face goes pale and I think he's going to fall.

It was pretty common those days. I quickly take him by the arm and gently lower him to the ground. He's holding onto me with both hands. He doesn't let go. I wait. I need to find a soft spot for his head and something to prop up his feet. But he doesn't let go.

"Dad, just let go," I say.

He looks at me with fear in his eyes, silent.

Leaning closer, I whisper:

"Dad, don't be scared . . . Just let go."

Dad slowly loosens his grip. And I lie him down on the earth.

13
Turkey at the End of Its Rope

I was around nine or ten . . . It's a hot September in Avanos. School starts in a week. All summer I've been in plastic sandals, hand-me-down trousers from my brother that mom adjusted to my size and a checkered, blue, short-sleeved shirt. A thick hemp cord around my waist that's called a *kendir*. "The breadwinners of Avanos wear a kendir," goes the expression. I am working in dad's *gazozhane*. The cold water runs down my little legs and out the cuffs of my trousers. In my pockets are the shells of pistachios I have munched on the sly. Dreaming of listening to "Children's Hour" at five o'clock on our Phillips radio. Fairy Soda from soda maker Mevlüt. . . The slogan was pretty naïve: "Drink fairy soda in the land of the fairy chimneys." That evening a relative was getting married in the open-air cinema. Maybe I would see Serpil. It was that time in my childhood.

In the middle of the day a strange crowd has gathered outside the courthouse on the public square. It seems like the whole town is there. Turns out the amiable old owner of the Merkez coffeehouse has been raping his dark, long-faced busboy, Ihsan, an orphan from a neighboring village, for the past two years. I always delivered our soda directly to their doorstep. One way or another the kid came to his senses and talked. Handcuffed and with police officers on both sides, the coffeehouse proprietor was hurried over to the courthouse with his head hanging. Hypnotized, the crowd watched them pass.

Suddenly our late relative Ismail pulled out a cobblestone and hurled it at the proprietor as he howled. If he hadn't ducked, that enormous stone would have smashed his head to smithereens, but instead it crashed into the gutter of the coffeehouse beside the courthouse. The image of that shattered gutter was lodged in my young mind and I would always think about it every morning as I wandered through town distributing our soda.

Four or five months later the coffeehouse proprietor went back to work as if nothing had happened. I thought he would never have a place in this world again but there he was back making teas, joking and carrying on with the regulars as he handed them out. Ismail, who had hurled the cobblestone, was back in the coffeehouse, too, playing *Okey* as if nothing had happened, now and then cracking jokes, too, with the people around him.

I never saw Ihsan after that. They told me he went to Istanbul to be an apprentice to a relative who worked as a tailor. I never left soda on the stoop of that coffeehouse again.

★

I am going to middle school. In the morning I wake up to the sound of mom working her loom and together we start the day as I have one more look over my lessons in bed. That morning mom has got up to do her morning prayers, splashes her face with water before she wanders about the room muttering prayers. At one point she approaches the window and carefully looks outside. In the empty silence of morning it becomes clear that a woman she knows is hurrying over in her slippers. For some time mom looks out the window full of curiosity and concern. I think I hear her say, "What in the world is she doing here at this hour?"

Toward noon they found the body of a swaddled dead baby at the base of a vine in the corner of a vineyard outside of town. I have never spoken to mom about that morning.

★

I have grown up ... Now I am a doctor. Ready to serve out my years of mandatory civil service.

After drawing lots for our posts most of my friends have ended up in health clinics in the east or the southeast, but I have been fortunate enough to get a post in a village clinic not far from Ankara.

Those were the most beautiful, most exciting, brightest years of my life ... But having said that they were also the times when I plucked diamonds off trees and stars out of the earth, years when I was blind to the notion of the impossible.

One day a group of patients had gathered outside my examination room like they always did every morning. At one point nurse Mesude hanım opened the door and shouted:

"Anyone waiting for a report."

Out of the crowd comes a middle-aged man with a beard and a seven- or eight-year-old boy at his side, hanging his head ... It's Remzi and his son Bektaş ... Wending through the crowd, they come into my room. It seems a relative has raped Bektaş, and was caught by the gendarmerie. They are asking me to prepare a rape report. I have to examine the boy's anus. His head bowed, the boy is silently waiting, the faint seal of the courthouse on this right wrist. When we have him come up onto the examining table and get on all fours and he looks up at me fearfully, my heart falls and for a moment I don't know what to do. The examination surely reminds him of what has happened to him. Then it is over and they are gone as quickly as they came. The image of the purple seal on the boy's right wrist is lodged in my mind.

★

Another day I went off to a village quite far away from town to perform an autopsy on a young woman who hanged herself.

Traveling with the prosecutor, I soon learned the young woman's story. Her name was Reyhan. She was newly married. Her husband was serving in the military when she was raped by her father-in-law and got pregnant. Her mother-in-law knows everything but stays silent. Her husband is soon to come back from the military so she is left with only one solution. The young woman hangs herself from a beam in their pantry.

The family has carefully followed the prosecutor's orders: "don't touch a thing until we get there." When we step into the pantry the first thing I see is the stretched-out, frail little frame of the young girl, her *şalvar* around her feet and the rope around her chin. A chair has toppled to the ground and beside it is her a bundle filled with a funeral shroud, soap, a washcloth, a loose robe and some jewelry. It's as if she has prepared for the trip.

Something else was hanging from a rope tied to the ceiling. A wheel of meat. Roasted in the summer and kept throughout the winter. It was traditional to keep this sort of thing hanging from the ceiling. Half of it was already eaten. Outside a group of villagers was silently waiting with a pot of water, ready to wash the body. When I got back to the residence that night I couldn't sleep.

★

Twenty-five years have passed since. Now I am in Istanbul. In the papers I read the following story: "Sahe Fidan from the city of Urfa, who was married off in a bride exchange, had an argument with her husband. Unable to bear a life with him any longer she took refuge in her father's home where she hanged herself in the bathroom, her year-and-a-half year old child strapped to her back." Those close to Sahe have said, "women married like this around here don't come out of their homes alive." And that's precisely what happened.

My dear Sahe, couldn't you have found another way? Oh you misfortunate girl, did you really think your baby would come with you when you tied him to your back? If only you knew the headlines in this country of mine, a country that leaves you no choice but the end of a rope? Your one-and-a-half-year-old dark-eyed son has stayed behind. Now he'll grow up in a country where hustlers and thieves are respected, jesters are applauded and conspirators and the unrepentant are crowned. My hope is that when he grows up to be healthy and sound he won't be mired in the pain and despair of a poor, dark-walled neighborhood of a big city.

A doctor of 25 years and I have no cure for a sister with no choice but to hang herself from the end of a rope ... No balm for Ihsan's loneliness ... Not the power to erase the seal on Bektas's wrist ... To listen to Reyhan even once ... I have nothing for them. And will I have anything after this? I don't know. My hope is that the people governing this country will one day wake up from this deathly sleep. My hope is that there will be a sliver of hope left behind for us ...

14
Hearts in the Palms of Our Hands

All the brothers and sisters were stretched out on the wool mattress laid out on the floor. It was really cold. No one dares to look out from under the blanket. Keeping my eyes shut, I listen to the sounds of my *ebe* from Cemel. I can make out what she is doing. Not long ago we heard the morning call to prayer. Now she is taking her ablutions before muttering prayers as she patters about the house. After kneeling down to pray she gets up and keeps moving. On the doorstep I hear the sound of a shovel and then a broom. So she is clearing out the snow. Now silence. Surely she has gone to the stable. A little later she'll come inside and go straight upstairs. To wake up mom. She'll nudge her feet to wake her so as not to wake up dad, too. Mom needs to get up but dad can sleep; because she will always spoil her boy. As she comes downstairs she is talking to herself:

"The sun is high in the sky and these guys are still asleep." By the way it's still five in the morning. A little later mom will come down to light the stove. Now my *ebe* goes outside but she's back in no time. Kneeling by the bed, she is up to something. Her hands are cold. Sticking them under the blanket, she wants to warm them up on my brother's feet. We all scream:

"*Ebe*, don't touch our feet!"

But her hands are frozen and she is determined to warm them up. I let her take my feet. To warm the palms of her hands. When I come back home from school my hands will be purple from the cold and I will put them in her warm, rough, wrinkled palms. Her weary palms whose lines have faded under the cracks of all the toil. Married when she was 17 and widowed at 20, my *ebe* always looked at the world with the innocence of a 17-year-old and with a great big smile stretched across her face. Her dad was my great granddad Ismail from Cemel, a poor sharecropper who worked on one of the fields that belonged to my granddad from the Köse family. When Köse Mustafa's first wife died and he was looking to get married again, my great granddad said in desperation, "Uncle Köse, I have seven daughters so take any one you like." Among them my granddad chose the youngest, Safiye, who was just 17 years old.

A little embarrassed my *ebe* used to tell the story: "As a dowry he pulled out a wad of yellow lira from a jug under his bed and gave it to your dad and said, 'take any plot of land you want from the wetlands'."

My *ebe* from Cemel worked all her life and without ever complaining. Boundless effort and compassion in the palms of her hands, she left this world behind and was gone.

★

I am very small. It is a summer afternoon. The kızılırmak is running through the center of town, babbling as it calls out to us. Keeping it a secret from mom, I go down to the river for a swim. It is one of those days when I keep my underpants on my head to dry before I get back home. I am walking with my head in clouds. As I pass the *kaymakam's* residence a young woman leans a little over the balcony and asks:

"What's that on your head?"

I hesitate for a moment . . . I think it is the *kaymakam's* wife and so I need to say something. In almost a whisper, I say:

"My underpants."

"But why are they wrapped around your head?"

"I swam in the river. And they have to dry before I get home. They dry out quickly in the sun. That's why."

I remember her flashing me a cheerful smile.

But I still wasn't going to be able to hide the fact that I had once again gone for a swim in the river. A mere scratch of a nail would tell all: no matter what we did a thin layer of mud was always left on our bodies after a swim in the Kızılırmak and rinsing in tap water didn't do the trick.

But this day was different. This time the trip to the river wasn't a clandestine operation. Dad has taken me and my older brother swimming. Now we are sunning on the sandy shore. A hot breeze drifts over our faces. Most likely dad has recently read something in the paper about Vitamin D. He is telling us about the benefits. Scooping a handful of water out of the river, he sprinkles it over my back. Rubbing his hand over my head, he washes my hair. Water dripping from his hand is fractured in the sunlight as it falls over my face and my eyes. How lovely. This was one of those enchanting days in my childhood.

After dad passed away I brought his body to Avanos. With tears in my eyes I washed him in the *gasılhane* of the mosque just next to that spot where we swam together years ago. The sun wasn't shining through the water falling from the palms of my hands.

I opened his hands and looked at the lines. I kissed those beautiful hands. Those hands that caressed me years ago.

★

Karşıyaka, Izmir. The air is heavy with the scent of magnolias and the sea. The pier is packed with life. I am wearing a thin shirt. Going to her work place. I go inside and stand silently beside her.

"Do you sell bathing suits? I need a bathing suit."

She stops for a moment, surprised.

"Alright then, but this is a woman's store. We don't carry anything for men."

"Ok, well then I'll buy something for a woman. Maybe a present for someone."

Later . . . Later we are in Bornova . . . An 18-year-old girl's smile at night. Çınar Patisserie in Küçükpark . . .

Two lines from a poem by Edip Cansever on the wall on which we sit side by side . . .

Then kissing the palms of her hands with the joy that comes from having heard her promise she would meet me the following day.

Then there is another girl who washes her hair every morning in the rain. In the Montrö Square. On my face lingers the scent of Aqua Velva. A friend's pair of trousers ironed the night before. A trembling hand that holds mine until I get to school. A day spent smelling the lingering scent in the palm of my hand in the amphitheater.

Years later perhaps a little note stuffed into the same palm. That's all.

★

September 12 is the day the king's soldiers start working overtime. Cleary they have made all the preparations well in advance. They chase us down as if they are out on a hunting spree in the forest. With their guns and their dogs. One by one they shoot the ones who lag behind, the ones who trip and fall and who are too tired to carry on. Calm in their cruelty, they corner the ones who can't get away and they take them alive. With chains, irons, clubs and cables they push the limits of their own villainy.

One of the thousands of stories from those who make it out alive comes from a brother in Avanos:

". . . I don't remember how many days had gone by. After a beating and the bastinado they picked us up and took us to another room. The told me to take off all my clothes. They drenched me in ice-cold water. I was numb from the cold. Right after that they started torturing us with electricity. There was someone else in the room. I knew the kid. From Ürgüp. They had him strip too. They attached cables to our genitals. Then they attached the other cable to our palms. They were going to shock us with a small electric generator. They told us what we had to do. When they gave me the first jolt I had to scream 'aaah' and when my friend was shocked he had shout 'eeee.' They made us bray like a donkey."

Such oppression has a devastating effect on prosperity. Everything these friends worked for slipped right out of the noble palms of their hands and was gone. And perched on their chairs like owls, they are left to live out their miserable days with a conscience that takes silence as their savior.

★

In those days I had nowhere to stay. Neither in the dorms nor in a friend's home.

After my last class I would while away the time in the coffeehouse across from the hospital with my satchel over my shoulder before I go to the casualty ward. Dressed in my scrubs, I was now an ambitious med student volunteering in the ward.

Some time after midnight I would slowly drift into the background and crash on one of the patient beds in a cubicle.

Many stories from those days remain with me as well as one harrowing brush with an emergency.

I remember it being one of those nights when the rain wouldn't let up. They brought in a pregnant woman who had overdosed in Manisa. When she came in she still had a faint pulse. The team in the ward administered CPR straightaway. The doctor and the nurse struggled for some time but they lost her. When it was clear nothing more could be done, there was a brief moment of silence. Then you begin to clear away instruments, devices and any medicine. The young woman's relatives are waiting anxiously at the door. Who's going to give them the news?

Leaning against the wall and waiting, I noticed a casualty ward nurse. Opening the hand of the young woman she had been struggling to save, she carefully examined her palm.

I gave her a look to say, "what's going on?"

"I have always wondered about the lines in our palms. I was looking for her life line. To see if it really was short?" says the nurse.

Filled with a strange emotion, I stepped over to the dead woman. I leaned over, looked at her body and then the palm of her hand. Right away I noticed her belly: she was pregnant. Her baby was no more than a month or two old. Now it won't live. Her mother had taken her. Now I was out in the world with the thought of a child without lines in her palms and my heart was aching.

15
The Burnt Smell Inside Us

Mustafa Usta had come to Fırınbaşı to fire the pottery he had piled up the day before. But first he lit a cigarette. On their way to school in the early hours of the morning students had thrown their modest backpacks up onto the wheat market wall and were showing each other "Yılmaz Güney" cards they got from packets of gum. That melancholy, end-of-a-holiday look was playing on their faces. Watching the burning ovens, I am on my way to school, dressed in my "he-can-wear-it-next year" jacket with dad's handkerchief in the inside pocket and a tie my uncle had tied for me that would stay like that all year.

When the fire from the oven got too hot, Mustafa Usta stepped over to a corner and lit another cigarette. A thick smoke rose up into the air and flames twisted like angry snakes as the fire hungrily blazed the jugs and crocks.

At one point the Usta caught sight of Ali from Hacı Bekir's family, who was wandering around the oven as if he was still asleep. Ali was a strange bird who wandered the shores of the river alone and never spoke to anyone. He didn't usually come to the Fırınbaşı so Mustafa Usta must have wondered what he was doing there.

"Ali, come on over here for a sec, come and have a cig," he calls out.

Without saying anything Ali slowly comes over. Raising his head he looks at Mustafa Usta.

"What's wrong, Ali? So early in the morning . . ."

The Usta hands Ali a cigarette so he can light his own and he takes a deep drag. He seems poised to do something but he stands there for a while, unable to decide. Mustafa Usta walks over to a pile of wood and chooses a log to throw into the flames now lashing out of the open mouth of the oven. He is suddenly startled by the sound of Ali's voice and he spins around.

"Allah!" Ali cried as he throws himself into the mouth of the oven. Mustafa Usta stood there for a moment in shock. Crock makers in their workshops, passersby and children playing in the ash all quickly gathered round. There was nothing that could be done when an oven is burning like that. And it burned for some time after that. Slowly the flames died down and went out. Hopeless and with not a little curiosity the crowd watched the smoke wafting out. It took a day for the oven to cool. Unafraid that they might burn their hands the crock makers then dismantled the oven before it was completely cold. They were looking for Ali.

A few bones among all the ash. Piling the crocks and jugs to one side, they would sell them in the Friday street market.

"Ali's scent was in our water and our food for weeks," mom said as she filled water into a jug she had just bought.

For years the scent of Ali was a part of village history. Over time the smoke that had wafted up from his body and that kindled a feeling of an infinite absence dissolved over the steppes and was gone.

Mustafa Usta's astonishment never ceased:

"I mean, it was simply unbelievable ... How quickly human flesh goes up in the flames!" he would say every time the subject came up.

★

"Come on, Adem, let's get the next one," said Yavuz Hoca and he disappeared down the corridor. We have a lot of work today, five autopsies to go. There is an Izmir sun outside, the kind that makes you happen for no real reason. Replacing the organs we have taken out of the last body, the technician, Adem, carefully stitched up the body. Then he stepped over to the refrigerator to take out the next one. Next is an old man found dead in the bathroom of his house in Basmane. He is tall, thin and fairly dark. They told us he was an alcoholic who lived alone. When his neighbors hadn't heard a sound from him for a couple days they broke down his door and went inside. They found him lifeless in the bathroom, his head in the bathtub. He had stored water at the bottom of the tub to use during water cuts. Drunk he must have knocked his head against the tub and fainted. His head falling into the water the poor man 'drowned in a handful of water,' to use Yavuz Hoca's words.

We planned to start the autopsy right away. But there was a problem. Either the refrigerator was playing tricks on us or Adem had missed something. The corpse was now frozen solid and we had to wait for it to thaw until we could do an autopsy. But we didn't really have the time. Adem wanted to finish everything before Yavus Hoca got back so he turned on the hot water tap and started to wash the body in burning hot water. Naturally the ice began to melt. But when Yavuz Hoca came back a little later he was enraged and we knew there was a problem with the hot water.

"What have you done, Adem? You have burned the man?" Adem just stood there holding the hose. We both stared at Yavus Hoca. Why was he making such a big deal out of this? In the end weren't we washing a corpse?

"My God!" the hoca kept saying as he paced about the room. Then it must have occurred to him that his reaction seemed strange to us so he muttered as if in defense:

"Do you know what it's like to suffer a burn, son?"

"For God's sakes the man's is being burned after death," he said and then turning to us, he added:

"Boys, a burn is an unbearable pain. Never forget this, when a patient is suffering from a burn think first of how you can relieve the pain."

★

During those years of mandatory civil service I also served as the doctor of a village prison. I would go on Tuesdays and if nothing else the convicts could look forward to that day of the week when they could sit down and have a nice long chat with a young doctor. Physical ailments were just excuses. I would finish all my examinations by noon, write any required prescriptions and then go over to the prison mess hall with the director. He was a hypochondriac and there was always some part of his body that was aching or going numb and he would hang on every word I said in response to his imagined condition. But most all I was curious to know more about the women's ward. It was only three by three meters big. And 11 women were kept inside. There was a young woman who always had a headache. She was nursing a baby. She had been sentenced with her mother-in-law. Every week her young husband came to visit. Sometimes I would see him planted at the door, holding a bag. Yet there was something strange about him. During the visit, husband and wife would lower their heads as if they were quietly waiting for the time to run out. Over the set meals with the prison director, I learned the whole story. Over an extended period the young man's father had raped the young woman. Neither her husband nor her mother knew anything about it then. But when it became apparent that the young woman was pregnant she told her mother everything. One night she and her mother killed the man in his sleep when his son wasn't there and set the house on fire. Word got out about what had happened. And they confessed to everything. Later the young woman gave birth in prison.

The young man was quiet, resigned. Every week he brought whatever his wife and mother-in-law had asked for, the same people who had killed his own father. And every time he met with his wife he looked helplessly at the child in her arms. He was just a kid who didn't know if this little boy was his brother or his son.

In a corner smoking a cigarette, he poured out his heart:

"What happened happened . . . There's nothing to be done . . . My dad got what he deserved. And I can't give up on my wife."

He saved what he could from the house. Clearly he was trying to establish a new life. A life you rub out only for it to be used again but the more you rub the more you reveal what was written in the past; strips of a parchment; a palimpsest.

★

"When I die will you wrap me in a blanket before you bury me, son?" dad asked me one day.

"Why is that, dad?"

"It's cold now and in the end I'll be in the ground. I'll get cold . . . And then there are all those creepy crawlies."

Of course I couldn't just say, "what difference does it make once you're dead."

"Ok dad. But for the love of God don't think about such things," I said slowly.

However I am still haunted by one tragic blanket story. On December 19, 2000, blankets like the one my dad had asked of me with startling innocence were thrown to young men languishing on their deathbeds for days in a cell in Bayrampaşa Prison. Listen how one of the soldiers who played a part in the massacre explained what happened years later:

"After the fire broke out in the cell we threw blankets at the inmates crying out for help, saying 'we are throwing in wet blankets to save you, wrap yourselves in them to protect yourselves.' 'But the blankets were soaked in paint thinner and gasoline and not water.' Wrapped up in them they burned even faster."

For 12 years the smell of burning human flesh has smoldered in the lungs of this country. The voice of that girl shouting at the bulldozer at the wall of the collapsed prison, "you burned them all," is like a palimpsest; you open a new page in your life to write down something new and it resurfaces. Either you turn away and slip back into a deathly slumber or you face the past and hold your shame accountable.

16
The Quilt

"I mean when exactly was I born, mom?"

"I have no idea, my lamb . . . Your *ebe* brought us a pole of grapes from the vineyard in Kuşadası. They had already dried. So it must have been the end of September. There was a carpet on my loom with a only a few days work left. Toward the evening I had contractions.

"You go to bed and I'll call your dear mother Pembe," your *ebe* said and then left. Karoğlan was playing just outside the door. Then Pembe ebe came. I gave birth to you right then and there. Your *ebe* cheered because you were a boy. Of course we were sharecroppers so we needed men to work the fields. Your brother ran to your dad to give him the good news. He was in Ortamahalle, playing *prafa* in the Hafı coffeehouse . . ."

"Dad, mom has given birth."

"Really, gave birth to what?"

"A boy."

"Oh that's all she knows how to do." Well, of course, after three boys the poor man was expecting a girl. How else do you think he would react? Despondent, my brother said, "He didn't even give me twenty-five kuruş."

"And then, mom?"

"And then . . . You were very weak. No bigger than a hand. I wrapped you in the blanket that was draped over the *tandır*. And I made enough *tatlık* to last the winter. In other words you grew up in a blanket . . ."

★

When they left their homes they brought with them "one enormous stallion, an old mare, an old carpet and two blankets." Or so mom used to say. In our new home I remember how she would weave at her loom day and night while my *ebe* folded blankets. Such labor and belief in the middle of the Anatolian steppes. In the mornings I would wake up to the sounds of mom at the loom and under the blanket I would do my homework for my classes that day. Those lines are forever etched in my mind: ". . . it is a dark climate. The summers are hot and dry, winters are brutal and cold. This is a desert climate. Vegetation consists of shrubs and low trees . . ."

"Did you write it down, my lamb?"

"Write down what, mom?"

"What I told you last night."

"I did, mom."

I had written down what she had told me in my blank yellow mathematics notebook. "Let us have loads of wheat this year. Let us have loads of wheat this year . . ." One hundred times. Behind me mom prays and there is a strange rush in my breast. Later I am leaning over the stone bridge, tearing up those pages and throwing them in the river.

The sixth of May. It's Hıdrellez. Mom has gotten up early and gone to the river bank. She will draw shapes in the sandy shore of the Kızılırmak. She'll make houses out of little pebbles and make-shift figures out of reeds. She will wish for her cousins to have children to raise, for her grand-children to have homes to live in and for me to go to university. It was probably Sunday because I hadn't gone to school. I had been lost in a book I couldn't put down for days. *Three Saplings in the Gallows*. Hüseyin İnan had returned to his hometown of Sarız as a fugitive. Birds of prey hot on his tail. Embracing her baby boy his mother didn't know what had happened to him. He was tired and needed to sleep. The blanket was too short. His mother is anxious, thinking Hüseyin might catch a cold.

"I will make the blanket longer," she says. "For the next time he comes."

"Don't bother," says Huseyin, "I might not come back." His mother doesn't know what he means. It'ss this spot in the book that always makes me cry, hiding under my blanket.

I graduated from Nevşehir High school as a nationalist but when I started university as a student in Politics I became a socialist. The reason was simple: That blanket that wasn't long enough for Huseyin's mother.

★

In an act of hardheadedness that was unlike me, I scolded health director Kemal for asking me to write him a prescription for his older brother:

"Where is the man himself? I can't do it unless I see him in person." Annoyed, Kemal said: "He's a little out of sorts, sir, hasn't been out of the house for a week. Doesn't go to work either." Opting not to drag this out, I wrote out his prescription for Akiton. Registered it in my ledger: "Paranoid schizophrenia. Prescription was given. Policlinic no. 654." I know the patient. Quilt maker Hamdi, I would always see him in his little shop on the main drag, his head bowed over a quilt. Lost in a world of colorful, embroidered quilts, he was a man who kept to himself. As Kemal left the room I said, hoping he would forgive me: "Tell your brother he should stop by and see me when he pulls himself together so that we can have a talk."

A snowy day. I am trudging through the only street in town. Serkan has lit the gas stove and he's waiting for me. There must be a patient inside. Serkan introduces him the moment I step inside, clearly trying to unload him on me:

"Hamid Abi is here, hocam. Kemal Abi's brother." So Hamdi the Quilter has decided to make an appearance.

"Welcome," I say.

"Thank you," he says, almost in a whisper.

A few telephone calls. The manager of the Post Office swings by for a glass of tea. A few patients from neighboring villages. Hamdi is still sitting there. Then he slowly opens up. I listen.

"Actually I came here to thank you. Sometimes I can cause problems for you . . . So thank you . . . For the medicine."

Over the following days he pops in more often. Sometimes I make the tea if Serkan isn't there. He obviously enjoys chatting with me. He is mostly sad about his wife leaving home, taking their only son with her. Quite often he brings them up. One day he comes to me with a large packet, which he gives me before he goes. It is a really beautiful quilt he has made himself. Sometimes he is nowhere to be seen, especially when he is having a "break down."

At one point he was holed up in his shop for quite a while. He didn't look good the last time I saw him. He was having more hallucinations, fits of delirium.

Around that time I went away to Izmir on an extended trip. Hamid spent some time looking for me. He asked Serkan. "He wasn't looking very good, hocam," says Serkan. The next day I was lounging in the afternoon when the new prosecutor sent for me . . . Someone has hanged himself . . . . We were off to a village some way outside of town. Apparently Hamdi hanged himself from a beam in a village vineyard house. I went and performed the autopsy. That night in the residence I couldn't get to sleep. Hamid's quilt was prickly. I folded it and put it away in the closet.

★

Istanbul. Troubled years. Now I was alone. When they handed over the keys to that 67-square-meter house I had bought with a five-year installment from Emlak Bank my doctor friend had pushed me to take, he said with the pride of a cowboy who had just gotten his noose around the neck of a wild horse:

"Aha so now you are on track . . . Only installments would tame you."

I called mom and told her I took the house. The following day she fasted. They had an animal they were going to sacrifice. For some time the only thing I had in my new house was the quilt she had sent to me in the back of a bus from Avanos.

I kept half of that wool blanket from mom's dowry under me and the other half over me. I used a chair cushion for a pillow. But a few years later when mom and dad come to Istanbul for Parkinson's treatment and they stay with me I rush out and buy a sofa bed and a TV . . .

Dad's illness is in the late stages. He is nothing but skin and bones. Fourth stage Parkinsons. Bedridden.

"This quilt is pretty heavy son, put something else over me."

"Of course, dad." I take my mom's wool blanket off his shoulders and replace it with a fiber one. He's really happy.

The day before he died he was coughing a lot. I went over and gave him a glass of water. "My back's cold," he said. "Tuck the blanket around me a little tighter."

"Can you get up, dad? And have something to eat?"

"No, son, just tighten up the blanket. I'll sleep a little. Wake up in the spring."

"What spring, dad?"

"Did I just say spring, son? I meant in the morning."

My dad never woke up again . . .

★

October 1984. Izmir . . . Ilyas was one of the last young men hanged by the Junta . . . Ilyas Has . . . A friend who had spent time with him in prison explains:

" . . . We were walking in the courtyard.

'So it's your turn?' I said.

'What turn?'

'They are going to hang you tonight?'

'Ah . . . You're right . . . I figured so much. I'm ready,' he said.

I touched his hair, and we said goodbye . . ."

Ilyas went to sleep in his bed that night. Wrapped in his blanket. Calm and comfortable as if he isn't the one they were going to hang. They came and took him away in the middle of the night. Just as they were leaving he put his foot against the door and said, "They will be held accountable for this." In the last letter he wrote before he died, Ilyas left a note about his personal effects. He left his watch, his trousers, his shirt and his blanket to his family.

I hear my son's voice in the other room. For the last few days he's had a fever. Today he is feeling better. But he's a little boy and he's always kicking off his blanket. I go in and cover him up. Later when I crawl under my own blanket I will quietly think about what I have lived through . . .

17
Where Are Our Dead?

We really tried but we couldn't bring him back. By the time I got there he didn't even have a pulse. He was a dark, fat man with a thick mustache. An intercity truck driver. They brought him in from one of the thermal baths that are so popular in Basmahane. When an attendant saw water running out from under the door he broke it down and went inside to find the man slumped over the basin. Clearly the man had had a heart attack.

I was in my second or third year in medical school. Those were my first days working ER till morning. I was fascinated by everything. It seemed every patient who came through those doors gave me the story for a film. After they finished filing the report on the deceased, they called for the nurse. She would take the body down to the morgue. I lingered at one end of the stretcher. The fact is I wanted to see the morgue. In a deserted hospital in the middle of the night we moved along the dim corridors. With a spine-tingling squeak of the cargo elevator, we arrived at the morgue. But there was just one problem. All the drawers were full. Grumbling under her breath, the nurse was opening and closing different drawers as she looked for an empty spot. She stopped and thought, then flipped through a registry book on an old wooden table for a while. She went over to a drawer, pulled it out and took out the body of a baby no bigger than her hand. She scanned the cooler for a moment. Then pulling out another drawer, she placed the baby beside the body of a woman.

Together we placed the body of the truck driver into the empty drawer. A strange grin stretched across my face, showing a mixture of fear and astonishment. I'm not exactly sure how I was looking at the man but the nurse felt the need to explain:

"She counts as a mother and so we've just put him in his mother's arms!"

"But will they bury them together?"

"Don't worry about that," she said as she moved to the door:

"No one else can take your spot in the ground. Everyone gets his own grave."

★

I am listening to the head nurse planted in the corridor. She is voicing her complaints about patients and the personnel working shifts.

"These attendants don't understand a word I say. The night supervisor caught them sleeping again. And the nurses on duty have been taking away packets after packets of ER cotton." She stood there waiting for me to ask her why. I was silent for too long and she went on as if overly ashamed:

"Forgive me, hocam, I mean I truly am ashamed to have to say this but, I mean, this is simply unacceptable . . . I told them not to tell the doctor, that he would be very angry about this. You don't know what I am taking about, right? Unfortunately that's the way it is. No matter how careful we are, sir, it just keeps happening. The new health official in ER spotted the activity and told me. I mean the young man's face was crimson. I mean it's shocking. At first I simply couldn't believe it. Then I checked and found out that it was true. It turns out they are using the ER cotton as sanitary pads . . . For the love of God, how could they do such a thing? ER cotton! Such gall. Well of course I took the necessary steps. I asked them to defend their actions . . ."

Soon the head nurse's complaining voice was a sweet bubbling in my ears. I have other things on my mind. Opening my eyes to give her the impression I am listening, I try to keep a displeased expression on my face. Then out of the corner of my eye, I notice a door to a patient's room off the corridor. For whatever reason it isn't completely shut. Through the crack I see a patient sitting cross-legged on his bed, I can see what he is doing. His hand under the mattress, he is looking for something. Yes, and he has it out now. A pack of cigarettes. He quickly takes out one and stuffs the pack back in its hiding place. A little later the door opens and out comes a fairly tall, dark-skinned patient on crutches. One hand is clutched in a fist. Without glancing our way, he slowly slips out of sight at the end of the corridor. Obviously he has gone out to have a smoke. I was curious to know more about him. When the head nurse came up for air, I took the chance to ask:

"What's ailing the patient in 302?"

"He is has 'Buergers,' sir. He has Engin Bey's disease. He's been with us for a week. From Dolapdere. But he's improved since. All the same we'll send him to Surgery. Necrosis in his right leg. I think they are going to amputate."

Buergers. In other words, 'Trimming Disease." Common with smokers. They are willing to lose a leg over smoking.

A little later the man comes out of the bathroom and walks past us, leaving a fresh whiff of smoke in his wake.

A week later they cut off his leg at the groin. I saw his relatives waiting for him outside the morgue. Had we lost him? No. "Thank God he's fine," they said. They were waiting for the amputated the leg. Truth is it hadn't occurred to me. "What are you going to do with it?" I asked. "We'll take it to the cemetery and bury it," they said. "You have to bury human organs, hocam, they also need a grave. They surely do."

★

I am in Avanos. There is that strange panic and stress that comes on the eve of a religious holiday. The weather is really hot. I am sitting next to dad in the garden, our backs up against the wall. For the hundredth time he is telling me a military story which involves his commander Semih. He ends the same way he always does, asking, "I wonder if Semih is still alive?" Then doing the calculations, starting from the year he did his military service to the present day, he comes to the conclusion that Semih must still be alive and then he moves on to another memory.

Mom signals to me from the living room window. She must have a problem she can't share with dad. Making an excuse, I get up and go inside, leaving dad in the garden. Mom is waiting for me on a spring mattress.

"Son, no one is listening to me so the least you can do is listen. Take me to Kıran. So I can visit the graves of mom and dad. It's been so long. I'll read them a prayer."

"Alright, mom . . . Of course, let's go."

Half an hour later we are at the Kıran cemetery on the hill overlooking town. Mom is looking for my granddad and my *ebe's* graves.

"The gravestones have all but disappeared. As if they were made of *kısır*. The wind and the rain have eroded the stones. Last time I came I brought some paint and splashed a little over what was left of the stones, leaving a mark . . . So I would be able to find them."

And we did. Mom kneels down like a little girl in front of the graves of my granddad and my *ebe* and she recites prayers and speaks to them. Standing a little behind her, I silently watch.

The next religious holiday is two months later. The holiday of *Eid al-Fitr*. I had both graves redone. And I brought mom for a visit. Weeping, she rubbed her hands over her face—she loved the new gravestones.

In her eyes I saw the same grateful look I saw in the eyes of an old man from Mardin looking at the cameras.

Seventy-year-old Ibrahim Aslan was shedding tears of joy because his prayers had been answered. Eighteen years later the bones of his son Emin had been found at the bottom of a well, which is why he was so happy. Now just lean back and think about this for a minute. A father is shedding tears of joy because the skull and the bones of his son who was murdered and missing had finally been found at the bottom of a well. In light of this all the other joys in this country seem profane . . .

★

There has been a military coup and the junta is keen to send people to the gallows to make a lesson of them. One of the victims is Veysel Güney. After attending two hearings, 11 days apart, he was sentenced to death and hanged on June 10, 1981. The Gaziantep Cumhuriyet prosecutor at the time tells about the night of the execution:

". . . I said, 'It is customary for us to ask. Veysel, what is your last request?' 'To write a letter to my father,' he said. We gave him pen and paper. He wrote his letter. No one there knew this man who was taken to the rope. No lawyer, no relatives, no one at all . . ."

Veysel doesn't have a grave. They weren't satisfied with just hanging him— they never relinquished his body.

". . . From afar came a crow with a dead crow in its maw and it landed nearby. It scratched away at the earth, placed the dead bird in the hole and then covered the hole with the same soil. Cain saw this and his heart ached and he felt remorse for having left the body of his brother out in the open and for not living up to the crow. Ah! It smarted . . ."

Hey executioners, hey butchers of pigeons, merchants of death . . .

We are already "digging the graves" of our dead before speaking, learning, knowing.

You have not given mother Berfo her son back; you have not given Veysel a grave . . .

Where are our dead?

You are not even a crow. We know that you do not even have the same shameful heart that Kabil had when he saw that crow.

But aren't you tired of circling overhead all these years, like vultures with dead bodies in your maws? If nothing be like a crow. Come down to the earth and leave our dead. Let them lay to rest in our hearts.

18
Mothers Sniff Out Their Lambs

I was around five or six years. May had exploded over the steppes in all her exuberance. The linaria, crocus and the evening primrose flowers had bloomed on the banks of the Kızılırmak and I was holding dad's hand as I watched him hurry hundreds of bleating lambs across the shallowest part of the river.

Each lamb was soon reunited with its mother. Suddenly the plain was a place of joyous celebration. The shepherd whistling, the lambs bleating and the river babbling. Such happiness.

I asked dad the first thing that sprung to mind:

"How do the lambs recognize their mothers?"

Pinching the ear of a lost lamb seeking its mother, he answered me without looking at me: "The mothers can smell them, don't worry about that."

★

Dad gave me a hug and breathed me in. I always remember his proud, upright way of walking. But now his shoulders were slightly slumped as he walked up the dirt road that led away from the school, without looking back, and then he disappeared. I was standing there stunned in front of the high school that had once been an old church, holding a plastic bag filled with a pair of pajamas we had just picked up from a fancy clothes shop, slippers, a toothbrush and soap. When I hug my own son now I can understand dad's despair then.

After finishing middle school I took the tests that allowed me to go to Niğde High School as a boarding student tuition free.

It was a Ramadan month. The older students were following the developments of the Arab–Israeli war on a transistor radio.

When the kids from Diyarbakır (boarding students who came at the same time as me) saw the cooked chickpeas at dinner they whispered to each other:

"Oh man, look, they cooked the chickpeas . . ."

By the third day I was curled up on my top bunk bed quietly crying as I breathed in the yarn in my hands. The zipper on my tattered old suitcase was broken and mom had tied it shut with the yarn she used to weave carpets. I had discovered that it smelled like her. In the nights to come I always slept with that yarn.

★

Severing my ties with Avanos, I had come to study at university in Izmir, and in Bornova there was a student uprising in the dorms. I had been wearing the same coat since I started in the Politics department and the same combat boots for the last 22 days. We were staying in a makeshift tent pitched in front of the little cafeteria. It was the most unexpected way to start my studies at med school. What do I remember from those days? Not all the rallies and the decrees. The one thing that has forever lingered in my mind is the scent of daffodil from the revolutionary girl, who was also in the med department, and whom I fell in love with at first sight.

I don't where she is now. But for some reason I will never forget those words said by our anatomy teacher, Ismail Ulutaş, who had the startling resolve to continue teaching us among all the conflict and the chaos.

"Before you actually examine your patient you should make your initial assessment the moment you see him or her at the door. Because every patient has his particular way of walking, a particular look and a particular smell."

I was under the impression that I got my first whiff of death from the cadavers in our anatomy class, but I was wrong. That's just the smell of formaldehyde. The real smell you get in the autopsy room.

It's a fall day and I am in my fifth year doing an internship in forensics. An entire family from Manisa has eaten a jar of homemade preserves made from eggplant.

But a powerful poison had come to life in the conserves: botulism. All seven of them died instantly. They had lined up the three kids side by side. A woman in a long black dress from the Aegean leans over the children, kisses them, breathes them in and keens:

"My lambs . . . My lambs . . ."

★

Only a few days left till graduation. It's the last chance I have to pass pharmacology. I am so stressed I am even thinking about dropping out. On the top floor of the house in Avanos I am buried in my notes, cramming for the course. At one point I step outside. I smoke a cigarette next to the pond. Reluctantly I pluck an overripe apricot off a branch—it tastes more like a *şekerpare* than a piece of fruit. Taking in the scents of the garden, I look absentmindedly at the swaying trees.

Slowly I go back upstairs. Stepping into my room, I notice mom inside, gathering up my scattered class notes covered in scribbles and medicine formulae, breathing them in and kissing them as she mutters prayers. Holding back my surprise, I watch her for a while. After kissing and breathing in my notes in the same way she does for the pages of our Koran, she sets them aside. In that moment I understood: I have to pass this test and finish school even if it kills me.

★

I am in Istanbul. Watching the gathering of the Saturday Mothers. Once again it's Saturday and I have Poyraz on my shoulders as I listen to a mother making a speech. Hüseyin Morsümbül's mother is talking about her daughter Fatma. Hüseyin was still in High School when his house in Bingöl was raided by police and soldiers, and he was taken into custody.

For 30 years his family has struggled to learn what happened to their son. Appeals written by his mother Fatma over the course of 31 years were never filed and then destroyed.

Hüseyin's mother always said:

"If I could only find the bones of my son I would carry them on my shoulders. How I miss his smell."

I feel ashamed of myself and I slowly take Poyraz down off my shoulders . . .

Not so long ago staff sergeant Mehmet Ciftçi was killed when a military vehicle hit a roadside mine during transport in Hakkari. His body was never found and his family announced that they wanted to be personally involved in the search. The mother of the lost soldier, Döndü Ciftçi, who was on dialysis for the last 30 years, said the following:

"Take me to my boy. I'll find him, I can sniff him out. Put me on a plane and I'll go. I beg you. I will look in all the cracks along the road, I can track down the scent of my lamb."

★

Sometimes I call mom out of the blue. Pressing the receiver to her ear, she says:

"Ercan, my lamb."

"Oh mom, how did you know it was me? Maybe someone else was calling, and that would be rude," I say. Mom:

"How could that be, my son. How could I not know? Your smell comes down the telephone line. The smell of Ercan . . ."

Mothers are such fascinating people? So strange. Unlike anyone else. But I'm sure they can recognize each other and they must have a common language we don't know and which they alone can speak and understand. Maybe they meet in secret and give each other news. Who knows?

Now what to say? And to whom?

Cruel monsters, fearsome merchants, proud statues, people with no conscience, oppressors!

Leave way for the lambs. Let them pass to the other side of the river.

Their mothers can smell them out. Oh yes they can.

Let these mothers embrace them . . .

19
The Soul of a Word

In her book Leyla Neyzi mentions a story by N. Kazancakis: Passing through a village two travelers pick a strange flower off a fence. A very beautiful flower. The village children gather round. The two travelers ask them:

"What's the name of this flower?" The children:

"We don't know but Aunt Lenio does."

"Run and call her over."

A child races off to the village center. Patiently the travelers wait and a little later a child returns.

"Aunt Lenio has died."

The travelers' hearts contract. They are not only thinking of the death of Aunt Lenio but also of the death of a word.

The soul of a word.

Words are not only a meaning that comes when certain letters are put together in a particular order. For example, the word "flower" is not just a physical flower. Or the word "letter." Is a letter nothing more than a piece of paper stuffed inside an envelope?

Why do we shiver when someone says the word "photograph"? Because it's more than just a picture.

★

For example, when you say the words compos mentis what comes to my mind is a little prayer book hanging around the neck of a frail, thin-faced child sitting silently between two gendarmerie on a worn-out bench that was gifted from the municipality in a long, narrow corridor of the health clinic. He left a neighboring town where he was working as an apprentice and came here. He took a rifle and right in the middle of the coffeehouse he killed his father who had been raping his little sister for some time. Now you have to examine the boy and write the report. Is he compos mentis?

Was he cognizant of what he was doing when he killed his father? Did he do it consciously and resolutely, and of his own free will? Everything you write down on that piece of paper will be a guideline for this unfortunate child, as thin as a branch, to determine how long he might rot in jail. So he is compos mentis. Aware and responsible.

A matter of distinguishing good from evil, the straight from the crooked.

So then I have a question for you: take a good look at your life and the decisions you have made. How many of us could write such a report with a clear conscience?

★

And then there is the "virginity test." Every time I hear those words I always think of those faint carbon stains our veteran secretary inevitably left on those tissue-like pages we used in those days, pages that were never unblemished, when I would go into her room to have tea after I had examined the patient. There is a mother waiting for me at the door with an indescribable fear swirling in her big green eyes, who tightly takes hold of my hands.

A family is impatiently waiting for me to write them a report after having come to my health clinic in a panic: During a trip to their hometown, their seven-year-old daughter fell off her bike and into a bush and when they saw the blood they thought she might have ruptured her hymen. In addition to the standard document, her mother insisted on me giving her a separate piece of paper that was signed, stamped and sealed.

"What are you going to do with that? There's no need to worry about this little accident, it's nothing. Your daughter simply scratched the top part of her leg. That's all," I tell her.

They are going to put the report in the bottom of her hope chest and when she gets married she will take it to her new home. Among the laced white pillows and embroidered tablecloths will be a report of "good health" for the life ahead of her.

Oh, those reports ... Oh you people peddling fear. Have you not once in your life spent a moment alone with your conscience? How long will you continue to wield power over the innocent, rose-scented bodies of our sons and daughters?

★

Words have souls. When someone says the words, "Battery Report," for example, I can't help but think of the disheveled hair of that boy brought in by two police officers. Though scrawny, pale and hardly able to stand up on his feet from the punching and the caning, he was tough as a nail. You struggle to get the cuffs off him, tell the police that you need to examine him alone, insisting on them leaving the room before you lock the door.

"Look, you can tell me everything. Believe me. Down to the last scratch. I am going to make them pay for this."

He pauses for a moment and looks lovingly into your eyes and says:

"Forget about it, Doctor. In any case they'll get bored and stop. I'll just go. But you should stay. If not they make trouble for you, write it down. No sign of any wounds or bruises. They didn't beat me ..."

Yes, there is still a reason to have hope in this world.

★

They are hauling marble out of a quarry some way out from town. Using dynamite to blast open the stones. It was either a misplaced brick of dynamite or a fuse that was too short. A worker gets pinned under a rock and dies. The others just barely squeeze out from under it. By the time we arrive with the prosecutor and his usual team, they have already pulled all the other workers out from under the rock and to safety. The prosecutor is now speaking with them while the autopsy technician rolls up the trousers of the worker who has died and prepares to cut them with a pair of scissors. A worker then steps away from the prosecutor and comes over to us.

"Brother, couldn't we do this without cutting the pants? His son is the same size. We'll give those trousers to him. He can wear them."

From then on what do those words "cordon off scene of the crime" remind you of? Will they take you back to an afternoon in one of those towns where you did your civil service as a doctor and wrote one of those court reports that you always had to write? Or will they remind you of the resignation of that laborer who was trying to salvage the trousers of his fallen friend?

★

Words have souls. These days there is talk of a *Feth-i kabir* to be performed to confirm the cause of death of a former president of the republic. For whatever reason, when I hear those words *Feth-i kabir* it's not that former president who comes to mind, but someone else. Zeki Erginbay was born in Istanbul in 1948. In 1967, he began his studies in the construction department of the Faculty of Architecture and Engineering at Istanbul technical University. Zeki Erginbay was a hardworking, self-sacrificing, patriotic young man of the 1968 generation. Following the coup of March 12, 1971, he was arrested.

After being granted a pardon and released in 1974, he took up a post in the Bureau of Construction Engineering (BCO). Zeki Erginbay helped publish the BCO magazine *Technical Power* and he served as its chief editor.

On a Sunday afternoon on January 23, 1977 he was abducted and, despite all search efforts, he was not found until February 2, 1977. They found his body at the Ömerli dam, a bullet in the chest. In a poem about him, Can Yücel wrote: "his rose-written body was all purple."

Some time after he was buried they performed a *Feth-i kabir* to ascertain the exact cause of death. The cause was made perfectly clear. Yet I really don't know if a *Feth-i kabir* does any good in a country plagued with so many assassinations that were never brought to justice. But if nothing else I know that words have souls. I know that all too well . . .

20
Three Kinds of Truth and Us

One

Being a doctor is like no other job. The people of Anatolia say, "When you are with a doctor there is nothing to be ashamed of." That's just the way it is. A patient steps through the door and suddenly tells you everything and it's all out in the open as she suddenly reveals to you the most intimate details even her spouse has never seen or heard of. Without hesitation she shares a secret shared with no one else and as if prattling on about any old thing. And stopped like that in your tracks, you suddenly become family, a friend, a confidant.

For example, it could be any old day when a frail, pale-faced, little woman with stomach pains comes in for an examination and, after she lies down on the examination table, you realize that she has wrapped a thick cloth around her stomach several times to hide her pregnancy, and that she will probably give birth that same day. Turns out she was more or less forced into a relationship with her roughneck cousin who drives a taxi, and the poor woman spent nine months struggling to conceal the pregnancy by keeping her stomach tightly wrapped in cloth. What would you do in such a situation? She's still on the examination table when her thin, graceful hands take your wrist and she says: "For the love of God, doctor, my older brother is waiting outside. Don't tell him anything, or he'll kill me." You have already become a part the story and you don't know how it is going to end.

Well here's what happened: she gave birth to a boy. I allowed for the midwife at the clinic to arrange a private birth at her home. The girl and her older brother then went to their hometown. I don't know the rest. But I know one thing: I pressed the midwife with one condition, that the boy would be named "Ercan." To that dark-eyed, milk-scented innocent boy who started out in this world with such injustice and misfortune, I could give nothing more than my own name.

Two

A bright Monday morning in the health clinic. In your crisp white coat you are waiting for new patients to walk in. Then the door swings open. A newlywed groom, almost swimming in his cheap suit, steps inside. Clearly he hasn't slept a wink the night before. He has no clue that one of his pant legs is caught in his sock. Beside him is a young woman clutching a "bride's bag," her hands adorned in henna. The people who have brought this couple in to see you so early in the morning are the old cobblers who work in the shop under the clinic. The old man's problem is this issue of the "bloody sheet." The whole family is up in arms. Since Saturday they haven't got the desired results. The reason: vaginismus. And no one was patient enough to wait. First you should tell the young newlywed how to treat his wife, how to undress her, how to kiss her. Without causing any shame and carefully choosing your words. Then it's the young bride's turn. The strange thing is how you are forced to face your own attitudes on the matter when you describe this "ideal relationship" and you can't help but feel a little ashamed.

A friend of yours who has spent many long years in prison is now trying to establish a new life for himself as a businessman. He has fallen in love with a married woman. Her husband is another loser who has had similar experiences. So she starts having an affair with your friend. Later the woman gets pregnant and gives birth. She tells your friend that he is the baby's father. But your friend sets off on a bender of doubt, pitching back and forth between belief and disbelief. When you suggest a DNA test to free him of his doubts, the answer only seems to point to the many psychological trappings of the human soul:

"In a way this is much better doctor. I couldn't bear living with DNA results. As the kid gets older and his face changes, I am always comparing him to me. It is as if every time I see him I am discovering him all over again, and myself, too. It's the strangest feeling . . . So like I said, this way's much better."

Three

A family you know has been waiting a long time for a grandson; and now the wife of their only son is pregnant and you send her to a friend of yours, a woman birth specialist, for tests. Everything is on track. Ultrasound results, blood tests . . . And to top it all off it looks like she's going to have a boy!

Then comes the day of the birth. Though everything appeared to be fine on all the ultrasounds, the baby is missing both legs: one from the knee down and the other from the hip. An anomaly at birth. Taking the disabled baby in their arms, the family leaves. A few days later mother and father come to visit you with their baby Emre. Nothing is said. When Emre's mother goes into another room to breast feed, his father gets up, puts his arms around you and you quietly cry together.

You tell him your story. How your wife was four months pregnant after her last ultrasound and your colleagues told you she should have an abortion. That day you and your wife hold each other and cry and decide that you are going to have the child all the same. Five months later Poyraz is born, fighting fit and in your arms and with a wild look in his eyes. It turned out they were wrong about Poyraz but they hadn't noticed what would become of Emre.

It is in the middle of a night shift and you are drifting off to sleep when a silent old man in his fifties or sixties comes in. He has recently picked up a cough and it just won't go away. After an examination and taking at an X-ray of his lungs, you notice the tumor. How will you find the right words to tell him? You are only two sentences in when he asks in a voice so calm it makes you shiver:

"Don't worry about it, doctor, just tell me, how much time do I have?"

You shut the door to the policlinic and slip into a deep conversation with the man, who is a gravedigger at the Zincirlikuyu cemetery. He has reached the age of retirement and he's just waiting the year out so he can get his last salary increase. From that talk the following sentence sticks in your mind like a nail:

"Who stays in this world forever, doctor. Do you know how many people these hands have put in the ground? Famous people and the rank and file, both rich and poor. Give me any name. I've buried them all. Their loved ones are fearful and they stay away. They can't go to the grave with them. But I am always there. I take the body in my arms and place him or her in the ground. And so you can't scare me with talk of death or the grave ... Go ahead and tell me, how much time do I have left?"

Us

Maybe this is a personal matter, too: Having the impression the world began with you and dreaming of an eternal life. It is why our skin has grown so thick. It is why our hearts are as cold as a bottomless well.

Living like that little woman who wrapped thick cloth around her body to conceal her pregnancy or like that man searching for blood on the sheets of a young newlywed couple and not in their hearts and with politics playing on the hopelessness of our young who have nothing left to give save their bodies and in our hypocrisy-laden system that deprives us of our minds that might have instilled the notion of "forward-thinking democracy" to our neighbors, we delight in a deadly drunkenness as we watch it all grow instead of cutting out the roots of the problems.

21
The Country Doctor

Me

I had finished my year in the town where I had been sent to serve out my temporary civil service duties and now it still wasn't clear how much longer I would be staying. I rented the empty tractor garage just next to the Central Restaurant and turned it into an examination room. A makeshift stretcher, a medicine cabinet and a Formica table—it was all I had. The Mayor who swings by for a glass of tea thinks the matter of my new "post" is no longer on my mind. He is rather pleased. He was going to send over his son, Serkan, a police chief, and says to me, "he can hang around with you and learn a thing or two."

It is lunchtime at the weekend. Anxiously I look down at the döner over rice the director of housing deeds has insisted on treating me. I figure he is planning to ask me to write a report for his sister-in-law. I had only taken my first fews bites when I noticed someone planted on the threshold of the open door. He was a big, sturdy man. Squinting at me as if he was trying to place me. Without moving at all he says with innocent audacity:

"Doctor Ercan, is that you?"

"Yes," I said, looking up from my food. He came inside, took a few steps over to the table and stopped.

"I've got tuberculosis, doctor . . ."

For some time we looked each other in the eye. I had learned that in situations like these I should let myself be myself instead of trying to normalize the conversation. Feigning sheer indifference, I said:

"How do you know?" And I leaned back a little in my chair. He took another step toward the table.

"Because I am spitting up blood, man. Blood comes right out of my mouth. I've got tuberculosis." He stopped for a moment then went on:

"What am I supposed to do?"

"Hold on a minute . . . We can figure this out right now."

Signaling for Serkan to shut the door, I got up out of my seat.

Pulling aside the velvet curtain dividing the shop, I took the man into the back. Considering this guy's great girth I couldn't believe that he really had tuberculosis. As I examined him I asked him general questions. He lived in a village some way from the center. He was a shepherd. Which means he must have spent years wandering about in the mountains. Why would he have tuberculosis?

"How is your appetite?"

"Fine. I'll eat anything!"

"Do you sweat at night?"

"Oh no."

"Have you lost any weight recently?"

"Nope . . ."

I stopped the examination. Stood across from him. We looked at one another. He speaks to me with this wholesome know-it-all air about it:

"But there's no need for you to examine me, doc. I have tuberculosis. I'm telling you that I am spitting out blood! Spitting out blood!"

Ah, of course. I realize I have skipped over the very thing I should have done first.

"Open your mouth then and let me have a look."

Using a tongue suppressor I had a good look at his mouth and down his throat. And when I asked him to open wide I spied something moving at the edge of his windpipe! And sure enough it was a slug that had set up camp at the top of his throat, moving back and forth. Out roaming the steppes he must have picked it up when he pressed his mouth against the pipe of any one of those fountains along the roadside and the creature was washed down with the water and got stuck in his throat. Sucking from that spot, it blossomed and grew. And every time the poor man tried to clear his throat he caused the area to bleed. The blood he was spitting out was in fact blood sucked out by that slug.

I wasn't ready to pay any attention to my teacher who had once told us not to try and scrape out a slug because it would just break in two. "Best is to have the patient gargle with salt," he said. Now I was excited by the thought of pulling that pulsating slug out of his throat with a pair of forceps.

"Serkan, now you hold the light for me right here. And try not to gag. Breathe slowly and keep your mouth open."

He did exactly as I told him and five minutes later I was standing there with a fairly long slug, which I had managed pull out in one piece, pinched at the end of my forceps.

"Take a look . . . This is it . . . You don't have anything like tuberculosis."

I drop the slug in the palm of his hand and together we draw back the curtain and step out. This strange look in his eye won't go away.

"Mother of God . . . So that was it!"

Suddenly cursing the slug he throws it to the ground and crushes it under his shoe. Then turning to me, he says with modest delight:

"They said you were a good doctor. God damn it, they were right."

Mom

". . . Clumsy Ahmet's grandson was playing on the doorstep. He gave the ball a kick. And it smacked me right in the eye. It felt like it was on fire. I'm telling you that's how it happened.

I thought I could see ants in front of my eyes, and no matter how much I rubbed they wouldn't go away. From then on I always had blurry vision."

Mom was actually describing retinal detachment due to high blood pressure but she had already determined the cause of her blurred vision: Clumsy Ahmet's grandson. I arranged for her operation in Ankara. When I finished with my work in town I went there that evening to pay her a visit. Every time I found her lying with her eyes closed in a ward with five or six other patients. Quietly I would go over to her and take her hand. Her eyes still closed, she would mumble:

"Is that you, my lamb?"

She stayed in the hospital for a while. Then I had her come and stay with me in my boarding house. I thought it would be easier to look after her that way.

For some time I was the only doctor in town. Whenever a new one came it wasn't long before he found some excuse to run away. It felt like I had been abandoned in the middle of the steppes. Like I had been there for a thousand years and I would stay there for another thousand. At the end of my first year I was already a devoted hunter and a regular at the city club. And whenever the mayor cracks open a new subject, I don't know if he is being serious or if he is joking:

"You can forget all about your next assignment doctor. You're from these parts now. Especially after we find a present-able girl for you to marry. Of course after that you won't be able to get out of your own house even if you wanted to," and the more such words spun out of his mouth the less frightened I became. The health clinic covered 65 villages and every day I had over a hundred outpatients. At night there were endless emergencies, follow-ups to do at sanatoriums, autopsies and all the reports to write ... I was beginning to fall apart at the seams and the worst of it was that I had no idea what I could do to change anything.

Winter that year was especially harsh. I had spent all day and evening looking after patients until midnight when I had to stitch up a farmer's finger he had nearly lost when it got snagged in some rope on a tractor. When I got back to the boarding house, I could barely stand. Moaning from the pain, I lay down to sleep on the sofa in the living room. Mom was quietly sleeping in the corner. The stove had long since gone out. There was an incredible storm outside. In a stupor I dozed off into bad dreams.

In the middle of the night I woke up shivering. I had a fever, a wild fear in my heart and rising palpitations. Sitting up, I waited there for a while. Mom had woken up and she came over to me.

"Mom, I feel terrible, I think I might be dying," I said.

"Oh repent for saying something like that, my lamb. What do you mean, dying? You've just been struck by the evil eye. That's all."

She left and came back from a side room with a fairly big blanket and laid it out on the floor. Then she took a blank prescription page off the table and with her other hand she pulled out one of the sewing needles stuck in the curtain. Curious and a little desperate, I watched her.

"Come over and lie down on this blanket," she said.

"What are you going to do?" I said. No answer.

Clambering to my feet, I went over and lay down face-up on the blanket. As she poked the needle through the blank prescription page and murmured prayers, mom circled around me like an American Indian. After five or six trips, she took a match from next to the stove and lit the holey prescription page. Reciting more prayers over the ashes, she sprinkling them over me from head to toe, and then she was done.

"Come and get up, my lamb, there's nothing wrong with you now," she said.

I got up and lay down on my bed. I felt pretty damn good. The shivering was gone and the fever was down. As mom went off to the bathroom to take her religious ablutions, I couldn't help but say:

"Dad was right. He used to say, 'son, your mother's a doctor without a diploma,' and I didn't believe him. But I swear, you're some doctor . . . It's just that tomorrow don't go and tell the nurses what you just did."

My words were lost in her prayers.

Dawn was about to break. The storm had broken and from the window in the living room the white snow was draped over the steppes like a perfect piece of clothing. Soon I would surrender myself to the arms of a deep sleep . . .

22
The File Under My Arm

It was my second day at the State Hospital. The first day went by in confusion and the to-do of all those phrases, "welcome," "will you have a tea?" and "doctor, please sit down, you're the guest today," until it was evening. Sitting down in the examination room at the entrance of the two-story policlinic, an annex to the town's little old state hospital I watched the way the old general practitioner Memduh, who came to the town every three months on a temporary rotation, examined his patients. As far as I could remember it was a Thursday and, as always, the town was more crowded than on any other day. People from the surrounding villages flocked to town for the street market to do all their shopping and, as if it was some kind of obligation, many simply had to pop into the state hospital for an examination. It seemed like that day would never end and that evening I met with the town bureaucrats at the only meyhane in town called Çiftlik that belonged to Hunchback Haci, and, pleasantly exhausted, I went back to my bed in the hospital which in those early days was home.

The next day I put on my white coat and with my fancy stethoscope dangling around my neck I had the look of a soldier about to enlist in the medical division of the army, ready to imitate certain names and titles I had learned the day before.

"Sırma hanım, is the tea ready?" "The stove is smoking again, Kerim Efendi." "Good morning, Şermin Hanım," "alright then, let's have the next patient in line."

I felt I needed to establish authority right from the start and that I should always keep a distance between me and the staff.

When Ertan Bey came into the examination room through the doctor's entrance toward noon, the routine that I had nicely set in place was upended. Ertan Bey was a local from town who used a large room on the second floor of the annex building as an office and who was called "Mr. Director," even though he was listed as a medical secretary. But for some reason everyone had accepted unconditionally his legendary appointment to the post of doctor and the clout that came with it. He was a strange, short, stocky man with a thick white mustache and bleary blue eyes and grey hair that he always combed back over his head who trundled about in a cheap, starched suit even though he was hardly ever seen detached from his chair and whose shoulders made this popping sound whenever he laughed.

Ertan Bey:

"Doctor we need to send your start report to the *kaymakam* today. Would you please come and see me." And slowly closing the door he was gone.

Brimming with excitement and a boundless joy, I examined patients and jotted down prescriptions until around noon when I heard our custodian Kerim, who was born with microcephaly, say:

"Ok, ok, it's noon now ... The doctor is going to have lunch ... That's it for now, come back in the afternoon ..."

A few old women protested but with a little pushing and shoving Kerim hurried the remaining patients out of the room.

When he came into my room a little later to put more coal in the stove he had a grin on his face with an expression that said, "and how was that? Handled that pretty well, didn't I?"

My head was swirling with questions: What was a start report? Where does it go and what do I need to do? I decided to approach Şermin hanım, who had been at the hospital for 13 years, pretending to be entirely indifferent about the matter:

"Şermin Hanım, Ertan Bey mentioned a 'Start Report' that has to be submitted to the *Kaymakamlik*, is that right?"

Looking me straight in the eye, it seemed a moment she had been waiting for had come and, emphasizing every word, she said:

"Yes, doctor, it is very important. And if Ertan Bey has already talked to you that means he has already prepared the report! You need collect the report and submit it to the *kaymakam*."

To give the impression I had understood everything straightaway, I said "alright then" and left it at that. A little later I noticed Şermin going into the office next to hers. It belonged to the environmental health technician Abuzer. They came back together. Flashing a row of large, stained teeth, Abuzer said:

"Praise God, doctor Bey, you've seen sixty patients before noon. Before we had Çetin Bey from Bursa. He managed a hundred fifty-sixty a day without batting an eyelid. But it looks like you're going to overtake him." There was a brief pause before he went on:

"Doctor, you should have Kerim Bey send the remaining patients home and bring over that start report. Otherwise you'll be late and there will be problems later on."

"Oh no, how could we let that happen?" I said with a shudder. "I'll go and get the report from Ertan Bey, alright?"

"Yes, yes Ertan Bey has already finished it," they all chimed together.

"You get it from him and take it over to the *kaymakam,* submit it there with a signature."

So I left without seeing the remaining patients.

The door swung open again and in came lab technician Serkan in a long white lab coat that was practically grey—he must have been wearing that coat for weeks. During my second week in town, Serkan got really into judo and karate and that's when I realized he was writing out random lab results when the lab equipment wasn't even working properly and when I told the head doctor in a state of astonishment and panic that Serkan was impulsively loading up machines that weren't even working, the doctor responded with, "fuck it. I know but what are you going to do if I write all this down? Either way the ministry hasn't sent lab material for months. And if we go ahead and tell them we don't have the equipment to do the tests then they'll open up an investigation with the subtext that we are the ones depriving citizens. So it's great, at least the kid is making something out of nothing . . . Hah hah hah." I was stunned.

Ripped with muscles, Serken leaned over and made eye contact with all the others in the room. For a fleeting moment, they looked at each other. Then he turned to me and said:

"Doctor, it seems you're going to the *kaymakam* to give them a start report, is that right? With all my best wishes."

I hung up my white coat, put on my jacket and went upstairs to see the medical secretary-cum-manager Ertan Bey. Putting some rather curious body language on display, he lurched up out of his chair, came over and held out his hand and said: "welcome doctor, won't you have a seat?" Sitting down in a chair, I got right to the point:

"So I'll just go straight to the *kaymakam* then. What do you say, Ertan Bey?"

"I have already prepared your report, doctor," said Ertan. "And I have placed it in a rather nice file. Now you know that this is a formal document. Here we give it a date and a number and then it goes to the *kaymakam* and from there to the governorship and then on to the ministry. You must know all too well that these matters occur along such a path. In other words this document is very important for you. In it I have put down everything we need."

As he said all of this, he was slipping various pieces of paper into a file the size of a briefcase that was covered in black cardboard.

As I watched Ertan he gave me the impression that he was putting into that file all the bureaucratic secrets pertaining to my professional life and my future.

"Now when you take this over keep it steady—God forbid something might slip out or who knows what," said Ertan and then he went on:

"You'll take it to them just like this, it is the customary way," he said striking a fatherly pose as he promptly stuffed the file under my arm. I was already up on my feet. Standing there with that file under my left arm, holding "all the power, majesty and mystery of the state," my entire body felt completely under its influence. Holding that file, I could almost feel the strength of the state and its warm compassion seeping into the marrow of my bones.

I walked down to the floor below. Nurse Şermin, health director Kudret, custodian Kerim, martial arts aficionado and lab technician Serkan and environmentalist Abuzer were all standing together, looking at me. On their faces I remember there was a slight twitching, something between a grin and a nervous smile.

"Goodbye doctor, and may it come easy. But heavens do be careful with that file," they said.

Leaving the annex of the state hospital at the end of the only street in town I started gravely on my way. At one point I reluctantly turned around to see the entire staff looking out a window, waving, while Ertan was watching me from a window in his office, as still as a statue.

Now I was a state official, a public servant. The file I pressed tightly under my arm was the first milestone on my road to a reliable future.

When Pharmacist Arif, who was drinking tea outside the Şifa Pharmacy with a few buddies from the surrounding villages, saw me he paused for a moment then asked over his shoulder, "doctor, what's up? Where to?" I had met him the night before in the meyhane.

"To the *kaymakamlık*," I answered with confidence. "I'm taking over my documents."

"Ha!" said pharmacist Arif.

"They gave you your file. Great news! But do be careful, your start report is very important. You mustn't drop it."

With a knowing nod, I went on.

I arrived at the government mansion that sat there at the entrance of town like an unshapely bulk. The *kaymakamlık* was on the fifth floor, the top floor of the building. Keeping a tight grip on my file, I hurried up the stairs. My left arm was now aching from pressing down on it so hard and the sweat from my armpit had slightly moistened its black cover. For a moment I wondered if my sweat had actually sullied my start report and I felt a jolt of remorse but I quickly realized I was blowing things out of proportion and I banished the thought.

The *kaymakamlık's* secretary, Vicdan, greeted me in a fairly bright mood, sitting me down in one of the old leather chairs before going inside to tell the *Kaymakam* I had arrived. Earlier that morning she had called to welcome me to the new post and managed to get me to write five separate boxes of the hypertension medicine her mother-in-law had been using for the past 10 years. When she came back, she wore a faint grin:

"Come in doctor, the *Kaymakam* is waiting for you, but please don't forget your file," she said as she led me inside.

Clutching the file ever more tightly in the pit of my arm, I went in to see the *Kaymakam*. I was meeting him for the first time. He hadn't been at the club the night before. His businessman brother-in-law Cem had a visitor from Hatay and the *kaymakam* felt it wouldn't have looked good on him if he'd left him home alone.

"Today is the auspicious day, doctor. Welcome, and may the job be felicitous," he said as he walked over to me.

No sooner had we shaken hands than I handed the file over to its rightful owner, the *Kaymakam* (!), proud of finally having presented this extremely precious and holy keepsake to him.

Astonished, the Kaymakam looked down at the file that I had pushed into his hands and then up at my face.

"What's this, doctor?" he said, the words tumbling out of his mouth.

"My start report, sir," I answered with full confidence.

"Yes, but why did you bring it?" And after a short pause, he asked:

"Did Ertan Bey send this with you?"

"Yes," I answered. He seemed slightly put off.

"Oh for the love of God, please have a seat," he said as he went back behind his desk. I knew something was wrong but I wasn't quite sure what.

He pressed a buzzer. A servant came in. The *Kaymakam* ordered two teas as he handed the servant the file as if he were relinquishing something disagreeable, and he said:

"Take these documents and have them process them."

Before our teas had even arrived he had finished signing all the forms on his desk without saying a word. Then putting down his pen, he leaned back in his chair and began:

"Doctor, you are now a government doctor. It isn't your job to shuttle back and forth with such documents. Now this ingrate they call Ertan plays the same trick on every incoming doctor so please forgive us. This is just some sort of game. More precisely, a scoundrel's game. I have no idea what pleasure he gets out of it. 'We'll stuff the file under the man's arm and totter him off on his way,' they say, and so what? Anyway, don't let it bother you, whenever there is another report send Kerim over and that will be that . . ."

The *Kaymakam* went on but I wasn't listening any more. I felt the shame and humiliation running down my neck and over my back, taking hold of my entire soul.

Swaying from side to side and with my tongue glued to the roof of my mouth, I left the office. Vicdan was busy with some other work, her head lowered over her desk. She didn't even look up.

My armpit was now empty. Not long ago it tightly held my file but now it felt like a great empty space that was grinning at me. My head bowed I walked the full length of the street. Passing Arif's pharmacy, I tried not to look.

Going up to my room in the hospital, I lay down on my bed without taking off my clothes.

23
The Country of the Forgotten Dead

Summer

Night is about to fall. Still burning the steppes, the sun does not want to set. After spending the entire day rushing here and there, tending to patients, I was planning to get away to the city club, the only place to have fun in town, when I was caught by the gendarmerie commander who invited me to sit down with him and have a tea.

Sipping our teas in the police station garden beside the local hospital, I am trying to convince him that garlic alone won't bring down his mother-in-law's high blood pressure and insisting that she should take her medicine, too, when his assistant comes over and says something to the captain. I can tell from the look on his face that my plans for dinner have just gone down the drain.

The mysterious death of a child in a nearby village. We hit the road. Me, the prosecutor, the fat court clerk, my taciturn autopsy technician and our driver all stuffed in one car, and the gendarmerie jeep trailing behind us. We arrive in the little village. There is a house with a big courtyard. A granary in one corner. The body of a child in front of a pile of hay, covered by a sheet. A bearded, old man on his knees, his face in his hands. Villagers huddled in silence behind him.

Grain hauled in by tractors is dripping out of the back of the granary. Unable to support the weight, the door hinge snapped and all the grain inside came pouring out. A four- or five-year-old boy playing in front of the granary was crushed under all that grain. Tons of harvested grain. No one saw him there. Everyone carried on working until they realized that he was no where to be found . . .

When I pull away the sheet to determine the cause of death, the old man, who was most likely his grandfather, stands up and, wiping the tears out of his eyes, takes my hands in both his hands.

"We have troubled you with this, doctor, and so late in the evening."

I mumble, "Of course not. No trouble. I'm just doing my job."

The prosecutor lights a cigarette and speaks with the others about the accident, asking only brief questions. I look at the court clerk and the technician to say, "let's get to it then."

The old man says, "Stop and catch your breath, sit down and drink some of our *ayran*." Turning to a woman in the corner, he says, "Quick, go and prepare a rinse."

The boy in front of the pile of grain . . . Like a doll, plump and beautiful. Not a scratch or a cut on him. Pure and innocent. Only a thin strip of blood running from his nose to the corner of his mouth. I touch his face and his body. He looks just like my nephew.

Meanwhile the ceremony of the *ayran* continues.

"Let's finish our work first. Maybe later," I say.

"What? You can't go on until you have your *ayran* . . . For the love of God . . . It's your first time here," says the old man. A little later I step over to the prosecutor, who is holding a glass of what they call a "rinse," yoghurt mixed with water, whipped up into cloudy *ayran*.

The prosecutor must sense my surprise because he says with an odd look on his face: "These folks are like that, doctor. A guest comes and they forget the dead."

I take a sip of *ayran*. The cause of death is clear. I say there is no need for a classic autopsy. The dark haired, rosy boy won't go under the knife. I leave him in the courtyard with a thin stream of blood over his lips.

Winter

Evening. When I breathe I feel a crackling between my upper lip and my moustache. Frozen, it's that cold. I dive into the deep, dark corridors of the Yücesoy Pasaj that sits in the middle of town like a monstrosity and which is still under construction even though the former mayor officially opened the building with all kinds of fanfare. I crouch over the stove at the entrance of head doctor Ferit Abi's examination room on the second floor.

Ferit Abi is inside with a patient. When he finishes we plan to go to a farewell dinner for the notary. Outside is a middle-aged man with a fairly young wife and child, about seven or eight, who is moaning in her arms. Now and then she leans over the child and mops the sweat off his brow. The father is motionless as he looks at them.

A little later a patient comes out. "Welcome Ercan," Ferit Abi says. "We'll get going right after I see this patient here. You just warm up there." And he steps back inside. Followed by the father, mother and child. I lose track of time as I drift off in the toasty heat.

Then there is a commotion inside. Glass hitting the floor. A crash. Ferit Abi is saying something like, "stand back, wait, wait. Hold on."

Then a long silence. I wait. The door swings open and the mother comes out in tears with her baby in her arms, a thin stream of blood running from his nose to the corner of his lips. The father's eyes are blood-shot, but resigned. Ferit Abi's face is white as a sheet.

The father turns to Ferit Abi:

"God took him, he's in God's hands, doctor. You're not the one to blame." Following his wife out of the room, he closes the door and is gone.

Earnestly I look at Ferit Abi's face. He mumbles:

"The kid had pneumonia. I thought I'd just write a prescription and send them on their way. Penicillin shots in his thigh, morning and night. They said they wouldn't be able to find anyone to administer the shot in their village so they asked me to do it. I had some pronapen here in the cupboard so I said why not. But the kid went out the moment the needle went it. Anaphylactic shock. I gave him a cortisone shot but he didn't come back ..."

We looked at each other with blank expressions on our faces. Then somehow I managed to say, "Well, thank God the family didn't raise any problems." Who knows where those words came from?

I was certain that the expression on Ferit Abi's face was no different than the prosecutor's that other day. In the same soft tone of voice, he said:

"These people are like this, son. This kind of respect stops them from seeking accountability when someone dies."

Spring

In the past the words "either a guardian or an angel" were written in old manuscripts. It was believed this prayer would safeguard the book against rain, fire and insects. And it was also rumored that the ink was made from the sap from buttercups, monksblood, which was a natural insecticide. In other words it was a kind of talisman written in special ink: meaning that there was a "protecting, vigilant angel ... ."

Why do we still fail to understand? The blood that runs from the lips of our children is like holy ink written as the conscience of our country: the burning sap that comes from their crushed bodies, the ache in our hearts ...

Either a guardian or an angel ...

For the love of the dark, hazel or green eyes of our children, for the love of their beautiful heads on frail shoulders just beginning to carry the weight of this accursed world, for the love in their hearts, these we know, all too well, are lighter than the wings of a swallow that has struck a window pane and died ...

Either guardian or an angel ...

Protect us from the enemy, from hate and oppression ...
From untimely deaths ... Protect this country ...

24
The Coming of the Fiancée

It was either the third or fourth month since I'd come to town. I had made a temporary home of an unused hospital room but after I moved into my new place it suddenly seemed like I was "living like a king." This was it, I could take a hot bath any time I wanted, boil water for tea in my kitchen and stretch out my feet beside a hot stove as I read my books. What boundless joy!

It was a tiny three-story apartment building. In the front and directly under me was the only meyhane in town, Split Salih's Şölen Restaurant. Split was the only black box in town. The nickname came from a split in his lip that he had from birth but was now hardly noticeable in his big face that was covered in pockmarks. Above lived the owner of the building. A husband and wife, retirees from the justice department.

I used the living room of my little two-bedroom home as an examination room and one room as a bedroom. The little room beside the front door was the "coal room." After stretching a thick piece of plastic across the ceiling, I filled the room with two tons of coal I planned to burn through that year. I hadn't taken janitor Remzi seriously when he first tipped me off, but whenever my mustache froze on even the mildest of winter days I was instantly reminded of the world I was living in.

Since last week I had been planning for Handan's arrival from Izmir. Almost every evening I would tell her which bus she had to take, where she would get off and which way she had to walk from there, but I was still anxious. According to the plan, she would take a bus from Izmir on Friday evening, arriving in Ankara that morning, and then find the number 21 ticket counter in the AŞOT terminal where buses leave for Kırşehir, and tell the people at the Mermerler Travel Agency that she was going to get off at Keskin when she bought her ticket, and of course she definitely had to remember to warn the bus steward in advance.

It takes about two hours from Ankara to Keskin so she would get to my place around 11 or close to noon. In detail I described the spot on the roadside where she would get off, the petrol station at the beginning of my road, the chicken farm and everything else. I explained to her that I wouldn't be able to pick her up there but that I would be waiting for her at home, and that once she got off the bus she should walk two hundred meters down the road and take the stairs on the left beside the restaurant that sold alcohol, which would take her straight to the door of my house. Suffering from a shyness whose origins still baffle me today, I didn't want the town to know I had a girlfriend. So after Handan and I spent the weekend together, Aykut, son of Naci Abi, who ran the bakery, would secretly pick us up in his Murat 124 and drop us off at the petrol station.

I got up early on Saturday morning and lit the stove. The house warmed up right away. Turning on the water heater I had put in last week, I checked the temperature of the water. Then I hurried through breakfast and pulled my chair over to the balcony door whose curtains were almost always drawn and sat down to wait. There wasn't a soul around. The cold winter we were having gave me the impression I was in the middle of nowhere. Apart from trips to the kitchen to top up my tea, I kept my eyes fixed on the street, peering through a crack in the curtain. I kept thinking to myself that when I see Handan walking toward the house I'll signal the front door to her from the window and maybe even meet her on the stairs before she has a chance to knock on the door.

At one point I got distracted creating an elaborate arrangement of sample medicine boxes in the living room medicine cabinet when there was a knock on the door. Thrilled,

I raced over. Yes, she had finally come. There she was smiling at me from the other side of the door. She was wearing her classic jeans, her sister's beret and the woolen cloak—the kind that were so popular in those days and which I'd bought with my first salary and sent to her—and she was holding a little suitcase—there she was standing right in front of me. Clearly she was cold. I quickly led her inside and shut the door.

"No one saw you, right?"

"Oh no. . . Nobody is out there. And I was the only one who got off the bus."

We had spent no more than an hour alone and I was on my way to the kitchen to brew another pot of tea when someone rings the doorbell!

Now who in the world is ringing the bell after I'd spent the whole week telling people I wouldn't be in Keskin over the weekend, making sure everyone thought I'd be in Ankara—I thought I had my story down pat. Was it a patient with an emergency? I didn't open right away, opting to wait in silence. But when the bell rang again I slowly and fearfully opened the door. Opposite me stood the waiter from Split Salih's place, Samet, who always dressed in shabby clothes and who was always grinning. He was fixed to the spot in that strange thing, something between a jacket and a uniform, that he seemed to have been wearing since the day he was born. He was holding a broad tray covered in thin paper, a bottle of water teetering at the edge, and on his face that same old grin.

Making my displeasure clear, I gave him a look to say, "so what's the deal?"

"Sinan Abi sent this over. Told me to bring it to the doctor. He says, bon apetit."

Hmmm. . . So Sinan Abi has sent me food. . . We stared at each other for a little longer.

"Fine . . . Come on in then and leave the food in the kitchen," I said, helplessly.

Samet breezed in and left the tray in the kitchen and with his head bowed he hurried out of the house, making a point of showing that he wasn't checking out the scene.

Handan, who had ducked into a room when she heard the knock on the door, slowly came out.

On the tray were two plates of lamb steaks, three or four pieces of *pide* and in the middle a little bottle of vodka, a bowl of roasted almonds and apple slices sprinkled with coffee on another large plate. Turning to my lover with a look of surprise, I said, as if I were talking about the most ordinary thing:

"Sinan Abi sent this over. He's a big fan. I guess he spotted you on your way here."

I went to the living room and parted the curtain. Pulling it back just a touch, I looked out and saw Sinan Abi, who runs the little corner shop directly opposite the house, raising a glass of rakı to me from behind his shop window.

"Cheers," said Sinan Saraçoğlu. He seemed to be saying, "You see I've known everything since the beginning, I've been watching. I saw everything, how she came down the street and went in to see you. I gave you a grace period of an hour or two so you could take care of your initial longings. Then I assumed you had to be hungry. I know which kebabs you like. You always drink rakı but this time you can have vodka. So you won't have bad breath. And don't think I'd overlook the almonds and apples sprinkled with coffee grounds. Cheers . . . "

By the time I had closed the curtain and walked into the kitchen, I had already understood that I could only really come to know this creature we call a human being in the best of towns, and that the experiences I would have living in such a place would leave deep marks in my soul . . .

25
The Lie

The first days of summer. I finished my work at the policlinic. Tired and worn-out, I'm on my way to the examination room. Serkan has tidied the place up and now he is standing outside the front door. I administer a shot to an editor-in-chief, who will only let me do it, and I send him on his way. Then the manager at Ziraat Bank swings by with *çiğ köfte*. He explains with great appetite how you have to eat them with just one hand. He's always in a good mood. Suddenly a tractor pulls up outside the examination room.

"Doctor, Hurry!" I see nine or ten people struggling to hold down a man on the trailer. The harder they hold him down the harder the man struggles. I climb up straightaway. I have to do something.

"Stop, leave him alone," I say. In that instant they all stop. I make eye contact with the man lying there. He is in his thirties. A thin man with brown hair. In a casual tone of voice, as if we've known each other for years, I say:

"Get up and come inside." The people stooped over him let him up. But they still look ready to jump. Pausing for a moment, the man pats down his clothes, comes over and sits down across from me:

"What's up? What's wrong?"

"Aw," he says, flashing a sarcastic smile. "I simply couldn't explain it. I've got this seed stuck in my throat but they won't believe me."

"How's that?"

"A good old apricot seed. One of them got stuck in there a month ago while I was eating in the garden. And it's still there."

"Could I have a look?"

"Come and look. You'll see it." I look. There's nothing. This is psychological.

Meanwhile the man keeps speaking to me with his mouth wide open:

"What's it like? You see it, right? It's sitting right there."

"Yes, I see it. Stuck in your throat," I say.

"Oh," he says, thrilled, and he looks around as if to say, "See, the doctor saw it. So I was right."

"Let's get it out then," I said.

"Ok then, let's."

I go into the back to wash my hands. Serkan comes over and I say, "Go and find me an apricot. Quick."

A little later he is back with the fruit. Taking out the seed, I conceal it in the palm of my hand.

Five minutes later the victim is holding the apricot seed I pretended to extract from his throat—an object nobody believed was actually there!—and like a victorious commander I raise it up in the air for all to see. Then I tell Serkan to bring us a round of tea.

★

A hot afternoon. I am looking out the window of my examination room. Villagers are coming to town early in the morning to sell their wares and buy whatever they need from Sümerbank. They are keen to hurry back to their villages before noon. On the backs of tractors young women and kids are sitting on sacks, boxes, cans of oil and the elderly are huddled under blankets in the corners. It looks like they are in a panic to get out of some forbidden zone they have been forced to pass through . . .

Taking my trusty stethoscope and high blood pressure kit and stuffing some morphine and an injector into my bag, I go outside.

I am going to Salih Abi's house. Salih Abi is in his fifties and he has recently retired from the courthouse. They gave him the diagnosis in Ankara. Lung cancer. Advanced metastasis. There was no hope. In front of his house is a little garden with freshly planted vegetables. Clearly he has green fingers. In the corner sit five or six beehives and on the doorstep there is a scatter of shoes. It's busy inside. Salih is propped up in bed, looking at the ceiling. Women are speaking to each other in hushed tones. Several kids are darting here and there. They spring into action when they see me. "Oh don't take them off," they insist, pointing to my shoes and I step inside. There is a sparkle in Salih's eyes. It seems like he wants to get up. Going over to him, I slowly sit down at the head of the bed. We look at each other for a while.

"How are you today? You look really good."

"I've been good for the past couple days. In fact yesterday I even had two bowls of chicken noodle soup. Though I shouldn't put this down to the wife's cooking. I think it's because of the serum you gave me. I think that's what helped." He pauses for a moment. "But today I couldn't sleep at all from the pain. I was a wreck in the morning."

"We'll take care of that. That's easy. I'll give you a shot now."

"But I understood yesterday, doc. Yesterday I thought I was going to get up. If only I wasn't so nauseous. And then now and then there's this pain. Otherwise I'm fine."

"Of course you are. That's what I keep telling you but you won't believe me."

I give him a shot.

I take a sip of the coffee they brought me. He's a little better now that the pain is gone.

Now I should drop the bombshell:

"So when are we going to eat some *tava*?"

"Don't you say? I can't tell you how ashamed I am about that. You know?"

"No, I don't, but tell me if you're not in the mood, otherwise I can have Mithat make some."

A little riled up and angry, he says:

"Oh give it up already, doc. You think I would actually let you eat Mithat's *tava*?" Ok, now I got him going. Animated, he went on: "If God wills it I'll be up on my feet. Then you'll have your *tava*. Now the sisters here could make you some but it wouldn't be the same without my touch. They never get the right mix of tomatoes, pepper and garlic. And you know how I treat the meat first. Lamb. Slightly fatty . . ."

As I slowly sip my cup of coffee, he tells me all about his recipe for tava . . .

★

I have come out to the front of the health clinic. Waiting for the bus to Ankara. Behind me are the silos of the Land Goods Office. Tractors and trucks are lined up in front of them. All loaded with wheat. The final days of summer. Harvest time. The drivers are quietly waiting, lying on their backs in the shadows of the wheels.

I am going to Ankara and I haven't told anyone. In the evening I'll have dinner at the club. Maybe I'll see Behçet then I'll stop by and see Oktay. Poetry. Rakı.

Someone is racing over to me. It's our custodian Kerim. One eye doesn't see too well—congenital microcephalous. I am really fond of him. In a panic he comes over to me but with his typical restraint, he says:

"There's a funeral, hocam. The prosecutor is asking for you. He is wondering if you were in your office."

My Ankara dream goes up in smoke.

In a funk, I go back to the Health Center.

A 12-year-old. The son of someone I know who works in the post office. Playing with his dad's gun, a registered firearm, the boy shoots himself in the stomach. He was on the brink of adolescence. A little fuzz on his upper lip. Now he lies there in silence. It is clear where the bullet went in but there is no exit wound. The pit is in him and I need to find it. It's important that the prosecutor match it to the gun. Drenched in sweat, I search for the pit. Nothing. I pull out the boy's organs. I can't find it. Now there's nothing left but his intestines. I ask for a bucket. Scrape out everything left inside. And then a ting echoes in the bucket. At last.

Carefully I put everything back, stitch him up and then clean up. The boy's father has arrived with a police officer. At front of the door, I say:

"I found the bullet right away. A case of internal bleeding, the boy died instantly. He didn't suffer at all."

He puts his arm around my shoulder. Together we smoke a cigarette.

★

One summer day I was in Bergama. I remember being there for a Psychotherapy conference. I saw his picture that the morning in the hotel. There was a notice beside it. "Honoring today our friend at his grave." Selim Martin. Selim. Before the 1980s. I am in Med school. Transferred out of the Politics department. Staying in a dorm. Something's happened. I go to his room, I want to talk to him. When I go in he's playing a saz. He puts the instrument aside and we have a talk over tea. I look at his clothes: He's wearing a brand new fancy suit, and I think to myself, how did he manage to find the time to iron that thing in all this mayhem.

He knows that I am from Ankara. We talk about how someone wrote "Revolution is the Only Way" on the roof of the Political Science building. It was the kind of thing that got you in real trouble. That extreme. After the coup in September 12, they killed Selim in his home in Bayraklı without even interrogating him. The news deeply saddened me. So now so many years later I would go to visit his grave in a seaside town. While we still had our lives ahead of us. What could we do but live? I went to his grave in Bergama, but I made it back in time for the last morning panel.

"Brother, your eyes are bloodshot, is something wrong?"

"Oh, I have allergic conjunctivitis. Sunlight triggers the allergy in my eyes. That's all."

26
Why These Scars?

Certain events can lead you up a road you can never come back down. There is turbulence and then a breaking point in your life and from then on nothing is the same as it was before.

You are a young doctor, just 23 years old. You get your assignment as a civil servant in a town in the middle of Anatolia, steeped in all the sadness and the heat of the steppes. In the middle of nowhere you are standing there with a prescription fluttering in your hand. It is as if you are lost somewhere in space.

You have been working for five or six months at a health center when a man who owns a funeral parlor comes in one morning and asks you to write a "burial report." On foot you set off for a poor neighborhood some way out of town—the family doesn't have a car or the money to pay for a taxi.

In the midst of incredible poverty you go through a crowd waiting in silence and come to the dead boy lying on a sofa in a corner of the room. His face seems quite familiar. And at one point you notice a prescription under a bottle on a little table beside the sofa. Straightaway you recognize your own handwriting. On top of that slip of paper is a half drunken bottle of cough syrup. Ok. So this is the boy with pneumonia you examined last week. You prescribed a heavy dose of antibiotics, too, but where are they? Didn't they work? Sitting down on the sofa bed in the entrance by the door to write your burial report, you slowly ask the father:

"You used all the medicine, right?"

The father pauses for a moment then speaks as if offering an apology:

"These days we've been in a bit of a pinch, doctor. So we figured we would get the cough syrup and leave the injections for later . . ."

And so after that day you press every prescription firmly into the hands of your patients. Especially those for children. Waking up in the middle of the night in alarm, you go over the prescriptions you wrote that day one more time. From then on you can't let a patient go until you ask him how and when he is going to get his medicine. From then on nothing in your life is the same again.

★

Then time passes. In a town in the Anatolian steppes six or seven years feel like a thousand. You learn how to forget some things. It's Eid and the hospital's head physician and your colleagues, a young surgeon who is on rotation and an old practitioner, have gone on holiday. You are bored and sitting in your office one morning when the head prosecutor's assistant comes in and tells you that you need to head out for a matter of justice. With the usual cast of characters, you head out to report on a fatal accident that has taken place in one of the fields outside of town. It must be July or August. The sun isn't yet high in the sky. It's the harvest season. Across the broad fields stretched over the steppes people are moving about like ants. Weary farmers stare at you with sleep dripping from their eyes as they pass you in tractors pulling wagons piled high with wheat.

The body of the young boy is lying in an uncut field of wheat. He is the son of one of the harvester drivers from Adana, who comes to the town every year to work night and day over these few months. He came to work alongside his dad, one of the harvester drivers who opted to work through the night to escape the unbearable heat of the day. Father and son worked two days straight without any sleep. Unable to bear it any longer, the boy went off to a corner of the field where he spread out his coat among the wheat and lay down to sleep. In the dark of night a tractor loaded with wheat never saw the boy and ran right over his head.

The owner of the field is distraught. He's concerned about the reaping of his harvest and wondering if he is now running late. And the prosecutor is quite unhappy for having been called away on the morning of Eid. He is of the opinion that there is no need for a doctor to do a classic autopsy and that everyone should just head home.

Stricken by grief and with a cigarette that is no more than a strip of ash dangling from his lips, the father is looking down at his son. A little further on the tractor driver is explaining something to the gendarmerie and the prosecutor.

Tired, you sit down on a nearby stone. Dressed in *şalvar* from Adana, his sun-burnt, olive face steeped in pain, the boy's father answers a question in a conversation running through his head: "People back in Adana were asking if we were going to sacrifice an animal this year so I should at least call and tell them that we did. May God take him."

Making your way through the golden wheat swaying in the morning breeze, you go over to the poor young boy. You are no longer the same person. For the rest of your life every breeze that blows over the steppes will remind you of this boy. Blood has stained your bread. Yes, from now on nothing will be the same.

★

Years have passed since then. Now you are at that age when you tell yourself that you don't surprise easily. From the middle of Anatolia you have come to the middle of Istanbul, besieged by Anatolia on all sides. In essence your life hasn't changed all that much. You are in a neighborhood made up of people from Sivas, Erzincan and Giresun. The same patients. The same problems.

You visit a village society group and hear the story of a family from eastern Turkey. The family marries off their 16- or 17-year-old daughter to a much older man. The girl has no hope but to marry him. Soon she finds the situation unbearable and she runs away. Her father, however, will not accept this and he takes her back to her husband. The girl runs away again. Since returning to her natal home is no longer an option she goes to stay with relatives who live in another city. They promptly inform her family and they come and collect her. Some time later she leaves for an entirely different city. Now she's going to look after herself. To the mind of her family, she is now living a wayward life. So her older brothers track her down and bring her back to Istanbul. Three brothers pack her into her a car and together they take a drive around the city. They don't know how to do it. Finally they come to the base of a viaduct along the highway. They tell the girl she has to jump. By now she has come to understand everything she has been through and what will become of her. She asks of her brothers only one thing:

"Brother, it's really high. I'm scared. Please just put something over my eyes. For the love of God blindfold me before I do it."

And do you know what happens next? Life becomes an uphill journey. That viaduct you pass every time you go to work in the morning looks like that hair-narrow bridge As-Sırat. Your eyes search for the silhouette of that poor girl on the edge, whose only wish was for her brothers to let her cover her eyes before they made her jump. Every time you pass that viaduct you get the same helpless, lonely feeling you get every time you pass by a cemetery.

You break out in a sweat. But for some reason you still believe in something. A breeze still blows over this world and it dries the sweat off your brow. It does every time . . .

27
The Municipality Man
Who Drew a Gun

It was in my fifth year of my mandatory civil service. I was in a little town quite close to the capital but it still felt like I was thousands of kilometers away.

I was tired and bored and I had lost those unadulterated emotions I had when I first started the job and worst of all I needed more and more money to support my new habit of whooping it up in the *pavyons* of Ankara at the weekend. It got to the point where the humble salary of a practitioner would not cover my nocturnal thrills.

Just around that time Ahmet Salcı, who served as mayor for a different political party every term, made a suggestion: "Why not have the doctor register as our official municipality doctor. We don't have one. Would you agree to being our contracted doctor?" Of course I jumped at the offer.

A week later I would sign up as a municipal doctor after a decision was made by the municipality committee. There was no need for me to join the committee meeting and best of all the municipality was going to pay me a third of what I was getting from the state.

In the beginning everything went well. The short, unshapely accountant to the mayor, Selami would stop by the health clinic at the start of every month, come right up under my nose and place a little envelope stuffed with money on my desk with a mysterious flourish, as if performing some kind of cloak-and-dagger act. He was always wearing a red tie and with spittle gathering at the corner of his mouth he hardly made any sense from the moment he started talking.

Selami was an organic fixture common in most village municipalities and public institutions—a local staff member who served in a fabricated post. For Ahmet Abi, who served as mayor ad infinitum, Selami was a villager, friend, and of course a confidant. I heard that the municipality's dirty work went through Selami, but whenever the subject came up I would say, "None of that matters to me, brother, as long as they pay me at the start of every month."

We had come to the end of a cold winter. Everything was up and running smoothly but something had taken the taste out of my mouth. For the last two months Selami hadn't brought me my salary and the worst thing of all was that I really needed the money that week. So that day I refused to sign the forms Şaban the Blind brought over for me and I scolded him before I sent him away.

"Tell Selami that the doctor wouldn't sign these," I said and I waited to see how Şaban the Blind would take my first salvo.

Grinning at me for a while with a blank look on his face, he left without saying a word.

The next day there was no word from the municipality. Truth is I felt even worse about the situation. These municipality people were just not getting it. The weekend was fast approaching and Haluk, son of Reis and I were planning go hear Perihan at the Elizi pavyon in Maltepe, but I was broke.

Unable to take it any longer, I called Selami. Though my tone was gentle at first it grew increasingly harsh:

"Buddy, send over my money. This is shameful. Don't you people have any shame?" And spouting similar accusations, I flew on now at the top of my voice:

"Don't send me forms and other boloney until you send my money. Only a coward would sign these now." And then I hung up on him. As usual Selami was muttering something I couldn't really understand, though I did get the sense that he was trying to throw the blame on the mayor.

A few days went by and not a peep out of the municipality when I left Mehmet the Kurd's Merkez Restaurant, where

I sometimes had lentil soup in the morning, and stormed over to the municipality.

In my turtleneck sweater, mustache and short black pea coat and the warm lentil soup in my belly, I felt a new confidence rising up in me.

I entered the accountant's office on the second floor. Selami was sitting at the end of the room, peering painfully through the files set in front of him with a stupid look on his face while his assistant Gülnaz, sitting at a neighboring desk, was struggling to adjust the corner of the umpteenth piece of carbon paper into the mouth of the old typewriter. When she saw me, she smiled and perked up. In a slightly flirtatious tone of voice, she drew out her words:

"Good morning, doctor. Welcome."

Pinching out a smile, I got straight to the point:

"Selami, brother, why aren't you sending over my money? How many times do I have to ask you? I told the president at the club, too. It's no problem for me to sign the forms but when it comes to the money it's all hot air . . . Is that it? Tell me if I'm wrong! After all, I'm the municipality doctor. You wrote it down in the books. You gave me a contract. You said this guy's our doctor. But this just isn't on, brother, a person should have a little dignity," and so I sallied forth as Selami listened to me in a strange silence, gesturing with his hand as if to say, hold on a minute, and then leaning over his desk he started to rummage in his bottom drawer. It wasn't long before he'd found what he was looking for because he resolutely got up from behind his desk and marched over to me. I was leaning against the frame of the door, turned slightly toward Gülnaz and babbling something about how I was right.

Then I saw the gun in his right hand and I immediately shut up. He came right up under my nose the way he always did when he talked to me. He was half my size but he reached out and grabbed the front of my turtleneck and yanked it up to my throat. At the same time he kicked the door shut.

Speechless, I looked at Selami with a mixture of fear, shock and desperation. Keeping a vice-like grip on my throat and showing a strength I'd never expect from a man like him, he pressed the muzzle of his gun into my temple as he pushed me back up against the wall.

"Enough already, you punk ... Money money money ... Well there isn't any, punk! Son, don't you just don't get when there's nothing there. I could just shoot you and be done with it, mother fucker ..."

My tongue was stuck to the roof of my mouth and my mind was a total blank, I was beyond fear.

Momentarily shocked, Gülnaz raced over to us. "Selami Abi what in the world are you doing? Brother, let him go ... Have you lost you mind, abi. Let him go already!"

"You want a bullet in the head, you want a bullet in the head," he said before he lowered his gun, batted away Gülnaz, let go of my throat and went back to his seat. Putting his gun back in his desk drawer, he said to Gülnaz:

"Girl, do I have any other choice? Everyone comes asking for money, more and more money. First it's the president then the motherfucking contractors ... And then the inspectors are hovering over me, watching my every move. We've got our head on the block so that everyone out there can have a good time. Not a soul has even asked, 'What's up Selami? Are you in a pinch?' We have a snake up our ass and we're trying to get it out when this brute comes over asking for his wages. I'm fed up with all already!"

Straightening out my sweater all scrunched up against my neck, I was thinking of my next move. Gülnaz looked strangely embarrassed and apologized.

"Doctor, please forgive us, this wasn't supposed to happen," she said or something like that.

Finally wresting myself from the spot, I whispered something like, "well I'll just be going then," and I slipped out of the room. Without making eye contact with anyone, I walked quietly back to the health clinic. Steeped in silence, I went on with my work without saying so much as a word to anyone.

I was in a confused, crazed and meaningless state of mind. Despite it all, however, it seemed a feeling of "simplicity" had taken root in me, something I had never felt before. That evening I went to the City Club like I always did. Opening the door and stepping inside, I thought to myself, nothing at all about this place or the people here has changed. Indeed the only thing that has changed was me.

As I walked over to the Ziraat Bankası manager's table, I saw Selami at the table beside him, drinking rakı with some of the contractors who were doing business with the municipality. He stood up when he saw me.

"Doctor, hocam, won't you sit down with us?" he cried.

As if hypnotized, I walked over to his table.

Selami:

"Now you aren't angry with us are you, doctor? We upset you a little today . . . But you shouldn't hold it against us any more . . . Hah hah hah . . ." he said, laughing.

"Oh no, why would that be?" I mumbled. And for some time we looked each other in the eyes. Then he threw his arms around me with a sincerity I could have sworn was real. I just couldn't decide what to do. Muttering something or other, I collapsed at the table where the Post Office manager was sitting and I ordered a rakı.

Selami turned back to the contractors and proceeded to tell them how I was an invaluable, first-class guy and how much he loved me, spittle spraying from his lips . . .

28
Tell All Your Friends, I learned How to Die

The other day an art director friend of mine gave me a call. He has a brother, who was an engineer. Bright-eyed and bushy-tailed. I remembered that he had graduated from Middle East Technial University, got married and settled in Ankara. Later we heard he had divorced and, like all the other young men who couldn't decide what to do next, he opted on the most important thing (!) and went off to do his mandatory military service; a month later he was in Hakkari. My friend told me that this brother of his wanted to see me and he said that it was "important."

Eren turned up a few days later. With premature wrinkles in his dark, young face and a glint in his eye that made him look even older, he slowly sat down across from me. This young man, who looked a lot like his brother, was thin as a whip. After some chitchat the conversation started flowing. In fact he did most of the talking while I listened. He spoke mostly about his ex wife.

"... *When I first saw her I was a second year engineering student. It was a spring day when I went to see a friend who lived in a little house with a garden in Emek. I knocked on the door and a young girl I had never seen before opened it. It was her roommate. I remembered how my friend would occasionally complain about her. 'So here's the beautiful girl in the flesh,' I thought to myself. Her name was Figen.*

For ten years after that I thought of her every minute of the day. Now and then I still read her old letters, the little notes she left for me in the mirror frame—I still carry some of them around with me today—and poems I wrote for her. It was like I had lost my mind.

Alone I couldn't fall asleep at night unless I heard her voice on the phone.

I never failed to kiss the palms of her hand when we parted and I'd keep something of hers with me so that I could remember the way she smelled. When I got close to home I wouldn't be able to stand it any longer and I'd hop off the bus early and run the rest of the way. We would hold each other in a long embrace ... For minutes ... Later we got married. In '98. I started working at a mining company and she became a reporter for a new magazine ... And then? ... And then there was 'litost.' Thinking back over everything we lived through till 2008, I was usually at a loss to explain it, until I came across that word. It's Czech. And it means loneliness, sadness, anger, disappointment, shame, helplessness, revolt and much more. A word that encapsulates all those feelings. In other words, a deep sigh. We divorced ten years after I went for those class notes."

Eren paused for a moment and looked at me with an awkward smile.

"In fact I'm a secret fan of yours. I heard about you from my sister. I read some of your stuff in a magazine that came out in the 90s. Some evenings I still read a piece by you from those days. Every time it gets me right in the gut."

He pulled a tattered photocopy from inside a book he had with him and handed it to me. I recognized the piece straightaway.

"... I know there's no point in saying it might not have turned out like this. It did. That's how it happened and let it be good news, tell all your friends that I have learned how to die slowly. The only thing left from those days when I ruled the world in my turtleneck and my bushy mustache is the memory of a pale-faced girl whose plans to leave me I had quietly put to memory; she is far away now and I will never hold her again. And it always pains me to think about her valise. Whenever she bowed her head, I thought of my childhood and whenever I leaned over to kiss her on the cheek, I was in Ankara, and when she clasped her hands and fell silent, it was Istanbul; and now I am left with a restless cold November rain that chills me to the bones and so many other things that have gone unsaid. She is so very far away from me now and yet she is all around me. You get me,

don't you? Now what do I have left but desperation? Where am I to go, what am I to do? Now the night is pressing down on me. Cold evenings when her letters no longer have any say, and bank accounts and dates are remembered and those phone calls to lick my wounds every time I drench myself in alcohol. This is all that's left. But there is also the good news, tell all your friends, that I have learned how to die slowly . . ."

Some stories are so similar. I handed him the photocopy.

"And then what happened?" I asked.

"I went to do my military service. I was a reserve officer in the gendarmerie," he said.

He drifted away momentarily . . . I watched him for a while.

Breaking the silence, I said, "How was the army?"

"Same as always. What else can you expect? I came back a year early. My old firm was after me. I started as a manager. It was a good job and I made good money. Moved into a villa in one of those new satellite towns outside of Ankara. I would come home late, mainly drunk, fall asleep under a blanket on the couch, and in the morning I'd quietly leave for work. I hadn't seen Figen for some time, no news from her. I'd heard that she married someone from her paper. The guy was one of the new rising stars. Had his own program on TV or something like that. One of those 'new world' types, the kind that makes you want to reach out and touch them to see if they're real but then a shiver runs down your spine and you pull back in fear . . .

One night I woke up to the sound of my cell, ringing and ringing. I looked and it was her, Figen. In tears she asked me to come see her. There was such fear and panic in her voice. I hurried out of the house. As I drove down that highway in the dead of night I tried to figure out what was wrong. When I got there all the lights were out and she was crouched beside a radiator, looking fearfully around the room in shock. She'd had a fight with her husband. The guy had punched her up. People in the apartment building had broken in the door. He attacked them, too. Standing there in the middle of the room, I looked at her in that state, my heart sinking. I put her in my car and we went back to my place. She quietly went into the bathroom. Spent some time washing up. Beside the window I had a cigarette as I waited for her without a thought in my mind. A little later she came into the room.

First she sat down on the corner of the couch. Later she got up, turned to me and said:

"Oh, could you just give me a hug?"

I went over and gave her one . . . Biting down on my tongue so that she wouldn't know I was crying. And I looked helplessly at my lost life, seeking a resolution.

After a long stretch of silence, Eren looked up at me.

"Hocam, hugging is actually really important. I wish we could have held each other like that before, I wish we could have given each other a proper hug. We never knew how much we meant to each other."

I don't remember how much more was said.

Eren said that he wanted to see me the following week and then left. It was quite late by then. I understood that my friend's brother was in fact trying to tell me so much more, and in a different way. I was convinced that after so much pain and suffering packed into such a short time this young man was left with a healthy conscience and a clean heart. But I was also left with the idea of a country that had forgotten how to hug. For in that embrace we are crying as we painfully look over those lost years, seeking a resolution . . .

29
God Willing, He Is Dead

I n my third year of my mandatory service I was sent to a town in province B. with a name that rivaled the town's high altitude, harsh climate and the cruel judgments of its denizens.

The truth is everything I had been through in the town before would help me out tremendously in B. In my first week they evicted the medical secretary from a residence he had been holed up in for years despite having no legitimate reason to be there, and I quickly settled into the lodgings with the odd bits of furniture I got from Sümerbank, and the carpet and the single bed with an extra mattress I got from Güven Mobilya. After making off with one of the unused stoves idling in a corner of the clinic and setting it up in my living room, I had all the furniture I needed.

I happened to learn that the *kayamakam* was from my home town and someone I dearly loved and he was as quick as he could be in getting me whatever I needed at the Health Clinic, and he took every opportunity to treat me differently than the bureaucrats.

I survived a fairly harsh winter conducting examinations in the Health Center, chatting over rakı in the city club and inspecting the small health clinics in the surrounding area.

One day I spotted someone bringing a tractor out of a little storage space next to the restaurant where I always had my afternoon lunch. It had been idling there all winter. So the man was clearing out the space. I asked him straightaway if I could rent it. By nightfall on the following day, I had already painted the place, put in a few chairs and a table, and I had divided the back in two with a piece of chipboard—in the end I had myself an examination room. Leaving the health center in the evening, I would go over to my examination room and sometimes read late into the night or chat over tea with people passing by; and, on summer nights in particular, I would examine patients from the surrounding villages.

It was a quiet, fragrant, cool summer evening. Close to midnight. I was sitting outside my examination room, my feet stretched out on a chair, leaning back comfortably as I gazed up at the sky. Suddenly I heard something in the distance, rapidly approaching. A tractor was barreling down the main road in town that ran to the villages. Reluctantly I pulled myself together and stood up.

I made out four or five people on the back trailer as it rumbled past me on the cobblestones. I sensed they were taking someone in critical condition to the health center on the other side of town.

Doctor Ferit from Giresun, who had the bad habit of getting everything wrong because he was simply biding his time till he got a post in Ankara, was on duty in the Health Center that night. Figuring I was in the clear, I settled back into my chair. But things didn't work out in my favor. It seems Ferit had left for Ankara without telling anyone. So there was no one at the Health Center. Five or ten minutes later the same tractor pulled up at my place. Health manager Erdinç was sitting next to the driver.

In the back a fat man lay motionless with a group of six or seven men and women crowded around him, pulling at their hair and beating their chests.

Grabbing my stethoscope, I scrambled up onto the trailer and, pushing the women aside, I kneeled over the man. Right away I knew he had died some time ago.

His people told me they hailed from a village that was 30 or 40 kilometers away and so it seemed unlikely they could have got a man who had suffered a heart attack out on the dirt roads to B, in time.

In quick and clear movements I checked his other vital signs but I nevertheless thought it was only right for me to perform CPR on the man to satisfy his relatives. I jumped to it. As I placed my two hands on the man's chest, two woman jumped at me, screaming, and I continued to pump.

"Don't crush him, for the love of God, don't crush the man ..."

As I struggled to fend them off, I continued to apply CPR, and I shouted over at the men:

"Oh brothers will you get these two off me!"

As one of the men tried to convince a woman to get down off the tractor, he said those words that would make my heart shiver every time I heard them:

"Come on, sister, let the doctor be so he can bring my brother back to life!"

10 or 15 minutes later I felt there was no point in trying any longer and I stopped CPR, jumped off the tractor and walked over to my examination room. With concern in their eyes, the men came over to me, waiting for me to say something. Sadly, I said:

"My condolences."

The sudden screaming caught the attention of people coming out of the nightclub and curious passersby and soon a sizable crowd had gathered around the tractor. I went in to wash my hands so I could prepare the death certificate. As I was telling Erdinç where he had to put the seal, he leaned over with a cigarette for me to light. No sooner had five minutes passed when a young man, who must have been a relative to the deceased, pressed through the crowd in a panic and stuck his head round the door to my office:

"Doctor, he's alive, my brother's alive ... he's breathing."

For a moment I stood there frozen. Tossing our cigarettes, we all went out. Now I was no longer the compassionate doctor who had done everything he could before grieving with the dead man's relatives, but a crap of a man who had failed, who didn't know how to bring this man back to life. In a flash I understood all this from the look in their eyes. Grabbing my stethoscope again I walked quickly over to the tractor. I couldn't help but wonder if the man had really come back to life. I jumped up onto the trailer. The man was still lying there in the same place, motionless. I leaned over him and listened. Around me was a deep silence and the expectation of a miracle. But no . . . There was no change in him, he was dead. But why did they say that he was breathing? Then I realized they had felt the mechanical release of air from his lungs, a result of the CPR. But then I thought I felt a strange fluttering in the man. As I felt for a pulse I must have pressed down so hard that I was detecting my own heartbeat, and I panicked. Had I overlooked something? What was I supposed to do now? If he really was alive was I late in taking the required steps? And if he was alive, what would his relatives do to me? These thoughts flashing through my mind like lightning, I jumped to a decision and told them to slowly bring the man into my examination room. The crowd immediately made room. The man was laid down on the makeshift operating table. His arms, legs and chest were all attached to a second-hand EKG. I switched it on. My heart pounding in my chest. Waiting for the machine to give a flat line, I prayed to myself: "Oh my God, let him be dead."

And yes, the EKG gave a flat line. Oh I was so relieved. I waited a little longer. A wave of relief hit me as I watched the paper flowing out of the machine.

"Aha, look . . . Flat . . . No activity . . . Your brother has died. He's now with God. What more can I do now?"

With a slightly resentful air about me, I handed the relative the EKG paper and went back to my chair . . .

30
Come Along, Let's Start off by Saving Ourselves

I t had been snowing around the clock for the past two days and I could barely make the trip from my residence to the health clinic. The village roads were completely covered. No sign of a patient or anyone else for that matter. Even the sun seemed reluctant to show her face. Every time custodian Kerim Efendi came into my room with that strange smile on his face to fill the stove with coal, my office was turned into a hamam. In such a snowstorm you could hardly walk across town. Electricity went out on the first day and it was only now back up and running this afternoon. What to do? During the day I kept writing letters. First to Izmir. To a few of my classmates who were doing their mandatory civil service there. To a friend who was forced to leave the country for Paris after the coup. And one to Nazif who left to do his military service because he was angry with everyone and everything, and of course a letter to dad.

"Son, keep the letters coming. When you're late your dad takes your last letter out of the cupboard and reads it again. And what's more he reads it like he's reading it for the first time. Your brothers can't stop laughing at the man," says mom.

Through the window I can see the courthouse car approaching. In his classic bouncy, good mood Salim the pay clerk gets out of the car. Whenever you see the man you can't help but feel that everything's right in the world. There is laughter in the corridor. Must be hamming it up with the nurses. A little later he comes into my office. Places a little yellow envelope on the corner of my desk. It's the extra money

I get when I do an autopsy outside regular working hours. In other words, "money from a dead man."

"The prosecutor says the doctor should get his things together because we're off to Yenişıhlı to do a recon and autopsy, if he's available of course."

"Are the roads even open?" I ask.

"They are, doc. The villagers have found the shepherd and they're expecting us."

Two hours later we leave our car as far as it takes us and we climb to the top of a hill. A group of four or five people waiting in front of a little cave come to life when they see us. Bending low, we step into the cave. His head bowed as if asleep, a nine- or ten-year-old boy is holding a stick with both hands, his back up against the wall, a cap on his head, wrapped in an old jacket. This is Kamber. A little shepherd in training.

Two days ago when the storm broke out the shepherd had managed to get his flock back to the village but Kamber trailed behind him as he rounded up the last lambs. Losing sight of the flock, he had no choice but to take shelter in this little cave. And without means to keep warm he eventually froze to death.

We bring Kamber out of the cave and lay him down. I am going to have them write up my official report. And then maybe do an autopsy. I check his clothes. Find a little knife in his pocket, the kind they sell in street markets.

"If he had matches he would have made it," says the prosecutor in a blank voice.

"At least he could have burned those twigs and sticks in there, warmed himself up."

Suddenly I was sent back to a childhood memory in Avanos. One of those days toward the end of winter when spring was just showing her face. Five or six of us went to Kıran to hunt for Keme. That is to say, truffles: those expensive mushrooms that grace the plates in fancy restaurants. In the first months of spring and especially right after a shower they would swell out of the earth near the cemeteries.

Poking at the earth with sticks, we collected the keme and stuffed them in our sacks. There was a sudden shower and we took shelter in a cave, one of many in those parts. Shivering inside as we waited for the rain to let up, the oldest kid in the group assuredly ran his hand over the wall of the cave. A little later he pulled out from a crevice in the wall eight or nine matches and a little med kit wrapped in paper with a pinch of salt. Soon we got warm around the burning twigs and sticks and we feasted on the keme in our sacks and the *keskiç* my mom had given us. When the rained stopped, we wrapped the remaining matches in the paper with the pinch of salt and put them back in the crevice before we left the cave.

That day I went back to the village a little more "grown up."

Years later I was studying medicine when I went to see the movie "Dersu Uzula" starring A. Kurosava that was playing in the Çinar cinema in Izmir Konak. In one scene, Dersu and Yüzbaşı are leaving a shack in a field where they had spent the night and Dersu does the same thing we did when we were kids. Knowing that at some point strangers would need the matches and a pinch of salt, he hid them in the shack. Watching that film I was reminded of our common humanity.

The prosecutor was right. "He would have made it if he had matches." That was true.

"No need for a classic autopsy. The cause of death is clear," I said, and this pleased both the prosecutor and Kamber's poor father. We quickly signed the official reports. Slowly I asked the autopsy technician if the road to Ankara was open. I might be able to go if we get back in good time.

We left Kamber's little naked body stretched out over the snow and his father, shouldering the bag that held his son's simple clothes. He looked strangely resigned as he wrapped his son in a blanket and took him away without saying a word.

My brothers.

I know those beautiful days of my childhood when I wandered fearlessly and without a care in my heart and full of the scent of evening primrose flowers are far behind me now. I have been tainted enough.

Now my neighbor's door is closed and locked. No longer can I freely swing by whenever I'm eager to gobble up some bread or raisins. I have lost the taste of watermelon and white cheese we would eat from a long table on summer nights.

Now whenever I pay a secret visit to the old stone house where I was born, I lean up against a wall and gently cry. It is now a concrete block. I used to lie under wild apricot trees in the village vineyard, losing myself in strange dreams, but those trees have withered.

But is the idea of keeping matches and a pinch of salt for others nothing but an empty dream? In this world going up in smoke, an accursed world whose taste is no longer on our tongues?

Do you know that this earth is a great dinner table and that everyone can benefit from it?

Is it so difficult to willingly set aside a single match and some salt without expecting anything in return, tuck them into a crevice in a rock?

Instead of consuming everything we could take only what we need and leave what is left for those who come after us . . . Is it really that hard to do?

Come along and put a pinch of salt and a few matches in your pocket and let's hit the road.

Come along as we shed tears for the world and for ourselves.

Come along, let's start off by saving ourselves.

31
A Whistle Out of Chestnut

Those were days when I looked at all the world with joy and wonder: They are shooting a Yılmaz Güney film in the area and a white car pulls up at the local gas station. We race across the football pitch to see him. The driver is standing outside, speaking with the halfwit pump attendant. In the front of the car sits a fat, stocky man with a James Bond briefcase in his lap. Yılmaz is in the back seat, daydreaming. He looks thoughtful and a little sad. Shoving through the people around me, I get close to the car. Everyone steps aside, impressed by my courage. My hands on the top of the car, I press my face against the glass and smile.

"Yılmaz Abi," I say slowly, "we love you, brother."

Staring thoughtfully into space, he looks up and smiles. Just like in the movies. The attendant closes the gas tank and the car moves forward.

"Yılmaz Abi, Yılmaz Abi," we shout with all our might. Through the back window, he waves as the car pulls out of the station.

A wooden bridge has been built a little beyond the stone bridge. Our mayor calls it, "our second Bosphorus Bridge." Munching on salted peanuts, I'm crossing this new suspended bridge with my old friend Ertaş.

"Now if they were to ask us on a test, 'who were the first people to eat salty peanuts while crossing this suspended bridge,' we'd know the answer right away," says Ertaş. We were studying for the entrance exams to the Science High School and everything in the world around us seemed like a question on an exam ...

Volkan Abi is running the open-air cinema. Every night I go in with a case of soda and I stay for the film. Sometimes I watch the same movie five or six times. Dad has expanded the business: We are now Fairy Soft Drinks Incorporated. When the master of ceremonies, Kara Mustafa, introduces dad, he says: "Straight from one of our own factories in town!" With a smile stretched ear to ear, dad has full confidence in the man. I'm thin, short, pale-faced and weak. I am a failure in physical education. I have to crawl over the horse vault and I can barely hold onto the chin-up bar. Dad takes me to a doctor in Nevşehir for a check up. Turns out I'm anemic and I have a heart murmur. Every morning mom fries a spleen for me on the stovetop and says it's best if I eat it a little raw.

"Bloody meat makes a hero you can't beat," she says, collecting the half-cooked giblets off the stovetop. My left ear is always filling up with water. But so what, I'm top of the class this year. The school principal, Rıza Bey, presents me with a Nacar wristwatch. "A Hislon would be better," says my older brother. My dad's childhood friend, Ali Doğan Abi, the oldest son of a bank manager, Uncle Hasan, has come from Ankara to stay with us. He's a student at Middle Eastern Technical University, and he knows Deniz Gezmiş. "You should definitely go to the science high school," he says to me. He's going to send me practice tests from Ankara. Ali Doğan Abi loves my mother's crock-cooked beans and he speaks fluent English.

One day a kid disappears in the river. All day his mom is crying on the bank, constantly searching for her son. Fanatics from Nevşehir beat the living daylights out of a kid from Avanos. My uncle is always talking about the Prime Minister, Ecevit ...

But at home dad is telling us all about the big event: "Our bottles are now going to be washed by an automated machine." How's that? The machine is due to arrive from Istanbul in a week. We're staring at the thing like it's some kind of spacecraft. Niko Usta shows up. He's a smart, thin man with a pointy nose. He stays with us for a few days. Straightaway he asks mom to make him *mantı*. Then he sets up the machine, gets it working. Places the bottles upside down on top of a revolving disk and pushes the button. The disk spins, the bottles disappear and a few seconds later they swing back around to us completely clean. A miracle!

Next day Niko Usta goes to Mustafapaşa in Ürgüp. It is the first time I hear him call the place Sinasos. It was his grandfather's hometown. They still have houses and cemeteries there. When he gets back from Sinesos, I see Niko Usta quietly smoking a cigarette in the garden. He stays like that for a while. On Niko's last day, dad makes a stew and we eat in the garden. Sitting on the edge of the pond, I'm trying to carve a whistle out of wood. I guess I've been struggling for some time. Niko Usta comes over to help. Taking the wood from me, he glances at my work and silently walks into the garden where he snaps off a branch from a different tree. Then he starts to whittle away at the wood with a sharp little knife he always carries with him. Not much later he comes over and hands me the whistle. In his sweet Istanbul accent, he says:

"Don't you know you can't make a whistle out of any old piece of wood?"

★

Whoever is ringing the doorbell isn't going to stop. I get up to see who's there. A tall, pockmarked man in a coat. He is standing there with an incongruously innocent look on his face, like he isn't the one who has been ringing the bell and pounding on the door for the last five minutes. A mild, innocent look on his face. It's summer but I get the feeling he's been wearing the same coat for years, like he's never taken it off.

With an odd dash of sincerity in his voice, he says:

"Where you been?"

"What's wrong? Someone sick?"

"The wife's sick that's who. We've been waiting for you since morning."

Clearly he's the type who comes into town at five in the morning, run his errands and rushes back to the village by nine. Behind him stands a thin, frail woman dressed in a long, black overcoat. She is quietly waiting. I go back inside to wash my face. We quickly walk down the only street in town, tractors passing us on either side, loaded with wheat. We pass the coffeehouse next to the police station, the sounds of a Karate movie wafting onto the street. Nine or ten people sit motionless in front of a television screen, half-filled glasses of tea in their hands. With me in the front, the man in the middle and the woman behind him, we make a strange procession, disturbed when a man rushes over to me. He has something to say but he's not quite sure how to put it. Tilting my head, he finds the opening and says:

"I took her to Ankara, and still no luck ... X-rays and all that ... Nothing ... They give her three or four different kinds of pills ... She's taking them, but nothing's changed."

"Ok, I'll have a look at her now. Tell her that I am going to examine her."

"Like I said, the medicine doesn't do anything."

I keep quiet and for a while we walk on in silence. Her head bowed, the woman is walking behind us, keeping the same distance.

The man starts talking again. Now it's obvious he's going to air his grievance. Decisively, he says:

"Well you go ahead and examine her but tell me this, is it going to be expensive? I swear I can't spend too much on this. In the end she never gets any better. So don't give us any more medicine if she isn't going to get any better."

"Oh come on, let me examine her first. How else can I know what's wrong?"

I understand from the way he's speaking that he's from a Kurdish tribe that was forcibly resettled in one of the local villages years ago.

We go into the examination room together. He's still talking:

"If it's going to be expensive, I'll have this one replaced, you know that? I mean if you really want to know, that's just the way it is. When they gave me this they told me it was good, got it? But that's not how it is. This one's sick. Always sick. So instead of wasting my money on this, shouldn't I just get a new one? That's what I'm saying. Better to just get a new one."

I examine the patient. Her body is weak, dehydrated. Seemingly oblivious to the examination, she calmly waits, her head still bowed. I can't find a logical cause for her complaints. But I'm thinking about what I can do for her.

"Your wife is in fine condition," I say. "She should take these pills . . . Vitamins . . . Look, it will do her a world of good."

Reluctantly he takes the prescription. He's clearly not satisfied. He looks at the woman. He looks at me then down at the prescription. He says something in Kurdish.

"What did you just say?" I ask.

He waves his hand as if to say, "forget it." But I insist:

"Tell me, what did you just say?"

As the man makes his way to the door, I hear the woman speak for the first time:

"He says you can't make a whistle from dry wood, doctor."

The man leads her out.

★

We have come to Yerevan to promote our movie *Once Upon a Time in Anatolia*. It's competing in the Golden Bear Film Festival. Yerevan is an ancient city filled with stone buildings. The festival organizers are always stuffing us with food and drink. When we get a free day, we head to the street market. I want to buy a whistle. In front of a stand, I'm looking over the objects for sale, trying to spot the good ones. A dark, big-boned salesman is quietly sitting on a stool behind the stand. I notice that he's listening to me speaking with my friend. Smoking a cigarette, he's mulling something over. He can't help himself and he looks up and asks:

"Are you Turkish?"

"Yes . . . So you speak Turkish?"

Without feeling compelled to answer, he says:

"Where from?"

"Istanbul."

"Istanbul . . . Istanbul . . ." he says a few times, and then as if speaking to himself he says:

"Hrant . . ."

The word tumbles out of his mouth, neither a question nor an answer. Just like that, a breath, a sigh: Hrant.

Strangely ashamed, I try to carry on the conversation.

"We love Hrant . . . He's a brother."

A sardonic smile steals over his face.

He is silent for a moment. Looking at his handmade whistles on display, he says: "You can't make a whistle out of chestnut."

I go back to my hotel with a dark feeling in my heart. No longer a young man, I despairingly race back to my childhood.

GLOSSARY

Kurban: An animal sacrificed to God at the religious festival of Eid, also used as a term of endearment.

Kızılırmak: The longest river in Turkey, the "red river" or Halys river that runs to the Black Sea.

Meyhane: A tavern serving traditional Turkish food and drink.

Feth-i Kabir: A postburial autopsy issued by court order in relation to a suspicious death.

Hoca: A religious official such as a priest or an imam, also a title used to show respect to an elder or craftsman.

Musalla: The altar on which a coffin is placed during the religious ceremony preceding burial in accordance with Islamic rites.

Somya: A small, single bed with an iron frame.

Parka: A dark green military overcoat commonly worn by leftists in late 1970s Turkey.

Abi: An older brother, also used to lovingly or respectfully address an older friend.

Pekmez: A traditional molasses made from boiled-down grape juice.

Anadol: A Turkish car produced in the 1970s, the name alluding to its birthplace, Anatolia.

Kaymakam: The highest-level state official serving in towns, the equivalent to a city governor.

Ebe: A midwife who personally oversees a birth or assists women specialists in large hospitals, also the title used to address a wise woman.

Tafana: A pantry in the houses in the old district of Avanos, near Cappadocia, where food is prepared and stored, sometimes used as a place to sleep.

Valla: A common exclamation meaning, "I swear," or "for the life of me."

Kadayıf: A traditional oven-baked sweet made of shredded pastry and pistachios.

Gasılhane: The place where a body is cleansed before burial in accordance with Islamic tradition.

Usta: The title for a master craftsman, also used to address a revered friend.

Yilmaz Güney: (1937–1984) Turkish actor, director and screenplay writer, known for such films as *The Herd*, *The Road* and *Hope*.

Hacı: The title used for those people who have made the holy pilgrimage to Mecca and Medina.

Prafa: A common card game played in rural teahouses.

Tandır: An oven in a hole in the ground, also a lamb dish slowly cooked over embers.

Tatlık: The cloth wrapped over the mouth of a *tandır* and which is often placed over a baby.

Hıdrellez: The holy day of dancing and feasting to mark the advent of spring on the 5th or 6th of May.

Kısır: A cold dish made of bulgur, also meaning, infertile.

Şekerpare: A small oven-baked sweet in thick syrup.

Ayran: A salted yoghurt drink.

Mantı: Traditional Turkish ravioli filled with ground beef and served with yoghurt and melted butter.

Yenge: The title of a sister-in-law, also commonly used to address a close female friend or relative.

Tava: A broad low-rimmed pan, also a dish of sautéed onion, peppers, tomatoes and lamb cubes.

Çiğ köfte: A traditional raw dish popular in eastern Anatolia, bulgur, ground beef and spices mashed over several hours.

Sümerbank: The bank founded in the early years of the Turkish Republic (1933) to strengthen the economy and which also operated a large clothing store chain.

Pavyon: An underground club with live music and dancing.

ODTÜ: A prestigious university founded in Ankara, known for its political opposition and where the 1968 student riots first began.

Keskiç: Homemade bread particular to the town of Avanos.

As-Sirat: The narrow bridge everyone must pass on judgment day to get to Paradise according to Islamic tradition.